Article 353

Article 353

TANGUY VIEL

Translated from the French by William Rodarmor

OTHER PRESS
NEW YORK

Originally published in French as *Article 353 du code pénal* in 2017
by Les Éditions de Minuit, 7, rue Bernard-Palissy, 75006 Paris.

Copyright © 2017 by Les Éditions de Minuit
Translation copyright © 2019 by William Rodarmor

This work received support from the French Ministry of Foreign Affairs
and the Cultural Services of the French Embassy in the United States
through their publishing assistance program.

Production editor: Yvonne E. Cárdenas
Text designer: Jennifer Daddio / Bookmark Design & Media Inc.
This book was set in Bulmer MT by Alpha Design & Composition
of Pittsfield, NH

1 3 5 7 9 10 8 6 4 2

LIBRARY OF CONGRESS CATALOGING-IN-PUBLICATION DATA
Names: Viel, Tanguy, author. | Rodarmor, William, translator.
Title: Article 353 : a novel / Tanguy Viel ; translated from the
French by William Rodarmor.
Other titles: Article 353 du code pénal. English
Description: New York, NY : Other Press, 2019.
Identifiers: LCCN 2018028886 (print) | LCCN 2018035269 (ebook) |
ISBN 9781590519349 (ebook) | ISBN 9781590519332 (paperback)
Subjects: | BISAC: FICTION / Literary. | FICTION / Legal.
Classification: LCC PQ2682.I316 (ebook) | LCC PQ2682.I316 A8813
2019 (print) | DDC 843/.914—dc23
LC record available at https://lccn.loc.gov/2018028886

Publisher's Note
This is a work of fiction. Names, characters, places, and incidents either are the
product of the author's imagination or are used fictitiously, and any resemblance to
actual persons, living or dead, events, or locales is entirely coincidental.

Nobody wants to fall overboard fully clothed into the ocean anywhere in the world, even close to shore—it's such a surprise for the body to find itself in this new element. One moment, the man is on a bench in a boat, chatting at the stern rail while rigging his lines, and the next he's in another world, with gallons of salt water, numbing cold, and the weight of wet clothes making it hard to swim.

Our boat was still slowly put-putting along, with little waves gently slapping against the hull. There were rocky islets in the distance that would soon be awash, while terns and seagulls circled overhead to see what we had caught, as if we were a trawler. In this case, a lobster and two crabs. Which is what was in the pot when we hauled it up, the two of us hoisting it over the rail—because there were still two of us at that point. People seeing us might have thought we were two old friends, as we raised the lobster pot together and checked the crabs struggling and beating against the wire mesh while we lowered the heavy pot into the cockpit. He was the one who pulled the lobster out and tossed it into the bucket quickly enough to avoid its claws, which started snapping at the plastic sides. Pleased as Punch at catching a lobster, he said: Kermeur, this is my first lobster, I'm giving it to you.

Today, I couldn't say if it was that thing he said or something else, but I know that not long afterward I was watching him flailing in the water, ignoring the splashes he was raising. Maybe he thought it was a bad joke. Maybe he thought he could make it to some rock or other that might be dry at low tide. Even the laughing terns perched on the sharp ridges of the few distant rocks jutting above the horizon seemed to think that what had just happened was normal, I mean a guy falling into cold water and trying to swim fully dressed, gasping and yelling to me for help: Kermeur, goddammit, come help me! Kermeur, what the hell are you up to? And he added "asshole" and "fucker" and "son of a bitch," thinking this would spur me to action. No dice; that was out of the question. I could already sense that even the seagulls, looking as white and cold as nurses because they never blink, even the seagulls approved. I've since thought that to really understand what happened at that moment, you'd have to ask a seagull.

I stepped into the wheelhouse and pushed the throttle lever, alone now at the helm of a thirty-foot Merry Fisher as if I were piloting my own boat, sitting in the leather chair behind the salt-spotted window, the crabs lying resigned at my feet. From the outside, I'm sure people would have taken me for an old fisherman accustomed to going out on his boat every day, silent by nature and spare in his movements, while the noisy wake behind me drowned out his screams. Then I pushed the lever a little harder, and with four hundred horses propelling us, the boat and I covered the five miles to the harbor in barely a quarter of an hour. You sure can't swim five miles, especially in water as cold as it is off our coast in June.

I moored the boat at the same place from where we'd taken it an hour earlier, Dock A, Slip 93. There wasn't anyone, or hardly anyone, in the harbor that morning, and I behaved as if nothing were out of the ordinary. I tied up the boat as if it were mine, climbed the iron gangway to the quay, and got into my car in the parking lot. Surely, I thought, someone would have watched the whole scene from a window or behind a curtain. In the car, I remember telling myself that at that moment the whole thing was being written with black ink in someone's observing eye.

I wasn't surprised when the police rang at my door a few hours later. I couldn't say if it was the gendarmerie or the national police, but there were four of them, two guys in uniform at the door and two others, a little more discreet, in the van parked at the end of the path. I must have a pretty guilty conscience to not be surprised to see the law swoop down on me like a vulture, already sinking its talons into my shoulders. And thinking back now, even if I'd seen them coming from afar, even if I'd spotted them on the highway with binoculars and figured they were coming for me, I wouldn't have done anything different. Even if they'd been following me since dawn, I would have done the same thing, heaved Antoine Lazenec overboard the same way and brought the boat back in the same way, following the channel to the yacht harbor while respecting the green and red buoys like railroad signals, with that seagull still perched on the boat's stern rail, maybe waiting for me to pay it to leave. As if the gull, with its round, unblinking eye, insisted on being part of the story, like an unshakable witness prepared to testify in any courthouse in the world. And I felt like telling the gull that I would go to the courthouse of my own accord, that I wasn't planning to evade the law.

I felt like telling it that I'm a seagull too, I glide above the water, aware that I don't have much flesh left, so I fly over the sea and the boats in the harbor, and I'm a seagull now, a seagull in the fog hanging over the port. I can make out the city starting to appear, but it seems written in a language I don't understand, an alphabet made of renovated buildings and open windows, and it's only on the ledges that I can see the crumbs that are left. Yeah, I'm a seagull and I'm also waiting for dawn, for people to put their garbage bins out on the street, because people here have learned that you can't put them out overnight, that you can't just stuff your rubbish in bags and toss them outside. No, you have to keep your bins inside all night next to your bed, to make sure no seagull comes and pecks them open. You have to live with the smell of your bins, the reek of everything prepared, digested, and discarded but that keeps on rotting beside you until dawn. That's the price of having seagulls around here.

With the police and the arrest, everything happened quietly. They said the stock phrases you use at times like that. I got my coat from the hallway and followed them without saying anything. I think it started to rain a little then, a windless drizzle that makes no sound when it hits the ground and even wraps the air in a kind of strange softness from penetrating matter and quieting it. Just as I was holding my wrists out to the cops as if it were an old habit, I took one last look around, at the ripped-up earth and the sea beyond. I told myself that I would have time to look at it, the sea, through my cell windows. Then the two cops shoved me into the back of the van and sat me on the plastic bench bolted to the sheet metal. It was uncomfortable in the van as it crossed the bridge, jolting at every pothole in a road worn by the weight of trailers hauling ten-ton boats. Looking through the rear window that the drizzle was fogging, you'd have thought the sky was trying to squeeze through the wire mesh to seek shelter too. It was like a sheer curtain drawn over the town—like our story, I told the judge—it wasn't fog or wind, just a curtain that can't be torn hanging between us and things.

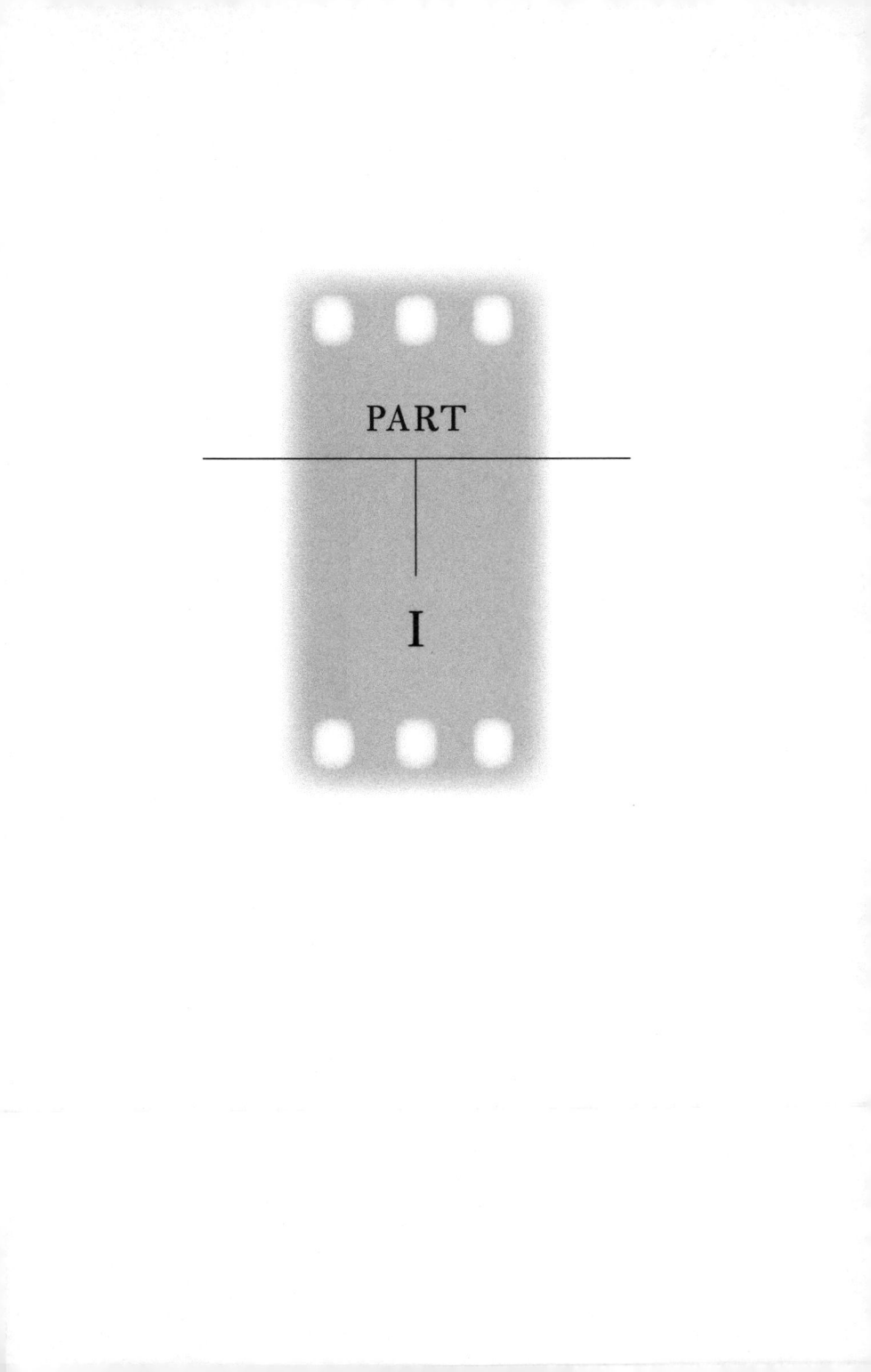

PART

I

So you came back alone, said the judge.

Yes. There were two of us, and yeah, I came back alone.

So you know why you're here.

Yes.

The body was found this morning.

I know.

The best thing to do would be to go back and start from the beginning, said the judge—without revealing if this was sort of a threat or if he was giving me a last chance. I was sitting on a wooden chair opposite the oak or cherry desk that seemed to elevate him a little, there in the one hundred and fifty square feet allocated to the two of us in the shabby courthouse office at the end of a dark hallway.

The sea breeze was still scattering my thoughts, the feeling that the windows were wide open, and that my thoughts—no, they weren't thoughts, images maybe—were still whirling around more than the wind over a sail. It was as if I were a cormorant aloft on a shifting breeze, scanning the sea for a tiny shadow or glint that would justify my diving to catch something, anything, so long as it was a place to begin, something sparkling under the water like the scales of a fish.

It would be nice to have these handcuffs off, I said. Me, I can't talk unless my hands are free.

The judge heaved a heavy sigh, a sigh that said, "I shouldn't, but I'm going to do it anyway," and he gestured to the policeman behind me that it was okay to take the cuffs off. For a *juge d'instruction*—examining magistrate—he wasn't condescending or harsh, and he didn't have the traits I'd expected, like a gray beard or a forty-year-old's paunch. This judge was thirty at the most and seemed like he wanted to hear me out. He could be my son, I told myself, and in a way, it would have been better if he actually were my son, given Erwan's situation right now—Erwan, that's my son's name, see—given the ten-by-ten-foot cell from which he was probably looking out at the town, since Erwan's screw-ups are part of this story too.

I rubbed my wrists a little to ease their soreness, and avoided looking at the gendarme because I didn't want him to think I was insolent or proud, since I wasn't proud of anything, no sir. And as the door quietly clicked shut, the judge gestured for me to start talking, his hands spread like a preacher's. The room smelled of fresh paint, that neutral gray that's often used on offices to hide their age, and it made for a strange kind of mixture, as if all the town's injustices had lingered there for centuries and were now trapped under the fresh paint, imprisoned for a long time. I won't say I was relaxed just then, but for the first time in months I felt like I was where I belonged. In fact, from the steadiness of my voice or my seeming to be at ease in his office, I could see the judge sit back in his leather chair and breathe more easily, as if to say that from then on he would be counting on me the same way he counted on the penal code.

From the beginning, Monsieur Kermeur, he said again. Take it from the beginning.

He looked as if he had all the time he needed. If it took two weeks, he would take them, if only to detect some hidden twist or turn in the story. So I said: It's about a run-of-the-mill swindle, Your Honor, that's all.

When I said that, I suddenly grasped the whole business for the first time, like I was taking a picture of it from the moon and seeing a planet wrapped in its big sheets of blue.

Just a run-of-the-mill swindle, I repeated, lowering my gaze to the wood of the desk with his hand resting on it, half hidden by dozens of files piled on the leather desk pad, many of them already labeled "Lazenec Case."

If we lived in a village up in the mountains or in some Wild West town a hundred years ago, I'm sure we would have seen him coming, I told the judge, maybe when he walked into town or rode down Main Street, spotted him from the stagecoach stop or the saloon, and it wouldn't have taken us long to size him up. And a hundred years ago, you would probably be a sheriff, with a revolver or something in your pocket instead of a law book you knew by heart, at a time when right and might weren't completely separate, if you can say that they've been completely separated since then, and if that's such a good thing, considering that power and violence have learned how to disguise themselves.

Anyway, the fact is we didn't see him coming. It was more as if he popped up like a mushroom under a tree and had grown pretty tall before we noticed anything. I'm not saying things were all that quiet around here before him, but in a region that probably hadn't appeared on TV in twenty years, most of the time life just goes on without any hiccups, with the usual daily stuff chewed over in the newspapers and bars, of course, but nothing likely to become the talk of the town. And then you felt like a rumor grabbed hold of everyone, and the rumor grew, and it had some basis, and worse, it spread and got into people, to the point where no one had more of a right to repeat it than anyone else. Like a kind of background noise that started gently rising, full of molecules that eventually rained down on each of us, without any one person feeling more guilty or involved or better placed to talk about it, but also without anyone keeping from adding their two cents or their anecdote and eventually their judgment, provided each sentence spoken could seal the guy's tomb, which we all would have liked to have closed over him a long time since.

No, not all of us. Otherwise, he would have never prospered the way he did, I told the judge, without our ever knowing who was really supporting him. And I'm in no better position to tell the whole story than anyone else, except that maybe more of the debris landed on my doorstep than at other houses, like shards of broken glass that some local wind picked up and blew to my place, the way newborns are left on certain people's stoops.

Seeing how long ago the courts should have gotten interested in his case, though, I'm only a new bud on branches that have been growing for a long time, I told the judge, a bud just opening on a November dawn as foggy as the streets of London, considering that when it comes to fog, England doesn't have anything on us. Maybe that's also why when a guy like him shows up with his straight talk and his straightforward looks, standing so straight on the damp ground, there was something about him that was like a hand reaching out to pull us from the waves by dint of energy and ideas about change, by big plans.

Because when it came to plans, he had them. That's the kind of guy he was, I told the judge, a guy with plans.

That's not a word we heard very often these last years, I'll tell you, considering who was around here, considering the five thousand somewhat tired people living on the peninsula. I can't say it happened more here than other places, but heaven's been hard on us for a long time, on the harbor there, the trails along the coast, the village streets, and even in the town council meetings, you felt the weariness.

So maybe all it took was a guy coming along with enough energy and a checkbook fatter than average for everyone to decide he was the one sent by some god or other to pull us out of our quagmire. At least that's what seems to have happened. The day he showed up on the peninsula with that simple idea of buying the château and the land around it, it was a little as if when he wrote the check that day, we all signed it with him.

I've never quite known why it was called the château because it really wasn't a castle, more a big freestone house with old slate tiles that were always sliding off the roof whenever the wind picked up, but it was big enough for everyone around to use that word, "château," since in a burg like ours, each thing has to have its own nickname to belong to all of us, so the house, which had been vacant for a long time, had also been called the château for a long time, perched up there overlooking the harbor, facing the city at the other end of the bridge.

We weren't the city, I told the judge. We were the peninsula opposite.

And we said château, first because being on the point there, it seemed to be standing up to the city. And I think we also called it a château because it belonged to the *commune*, the municipality. In fact, it was because it belonged to the commune that they needed someone to maintain the grounds, someone to mow the five acres of lawn once a month as if it were a real castle, so they needed a groundskeeper. And in a way, I was that groundskeeper, at least from when the mayor at the time offered me the job—Something to tide you over, he'd said—because of the troubles that were raining down on me in those years, so maybe out of friendship, and maybe compassion, too, he suggested that I look after the château and live in the little empty house at the entrance to the estate.

In exchange, you'll just have to maintain the grounds, Le Goff told me—the mayor's name was Le Goff, see. He was offering me a place to live and all I had to do was mow the grass and trim the hedges, and when the place was eventually put up for sale (given the commune's finances, that was the plan, to sell the château someday), I would show people around. I still remember how he came to see me one evening to give me the news. After we'd swapped a few remarks about the drizzle coming down, he looked at the ground and muttered, as if it cost him more than me: So we're going to sell.

And I asked him, As is? You want to sell it as is?

Yeah, as is, we're selling it and we aren't touching a thing, we're leaving everything, along with the spiders who've spun their webs and the resident ghosts, whoever buys it gets everything.

So I said: What about me? Will I have to leave?

It won't change anything for you, Kermeur, you'll just have to make an arrangement with the new owner, because the five acres will belong to him.

Then he added, And if your finances improve, then…

I knew very well what he meant, and he knew very well that I knew that my finances were due to get a lot better very soon, as soon as I got the layoff bonus from the Arsenal shipyards. It would be a fresh start for me, for me and a few thousand other guys, since in the last three years they'd laid off four-fifths of the workers.

The Arsenal will be closed in less than ten years, I told the judge. In less than ten years, it'll be nothing but a memorial downtown. Maybe there'll still be high fences and cops at the gate to keep people out. Maybe people will wonder what's going on inside. But it will actually be empty, all that'll be left are forgotten motions, dusty machines, and missing workers. I'm not saying it's good or bad, just that it hit us pretty fast. But all those quick layoffs didn't cause much of a stir, much less strikes or protests, for the simple reason that for once the city or state government, or both of them, didn't quibble about the layoff terms. Everyone got an average of four hundred thousand francs as a separation bonus, and you have to think what four hundred thousand francs meant in 1990. It was the price of a little house here in Finistère.

Even the shop stewards and the militants had to admit how smoothly the slow, eventual closing of the shipyard was happening. Most of us, the moment we were laid off, started spending our time reading real estate listings or looking at boats in showroom windows, not haggling over an extra twenty thousand francs.

Still today, when you walk the coast trails high over the ocean, even during the week, you'll see a lot of guys who look too young to be retired standing tall at the helm of their fishing boats out in the channel, fighting the current and the waves kicked up by a contrary wind, and later proudly spreading their catch on the dock, because in the ten years since they were laid off they had to do something to occupy their mornings—mornings, because you have to get up early if you want to go fishing, see, and haul up your pots before someone does it for you. But I better not start talking about fishing, I told the judge, because there'll be no stopping me, and anyway, that's not why I'm here.

That remains to be seen, said the judge.

I didn't answer, because I don't have that gift that judges and lawyers have, of firing words into the air like cracking a whip. Anyway, it's not as if I hadn't told myself a thousand times that with the money, I too should buy myself a good fishing boat with a motor powerful enough to get through the waves at the harbor entrance. Also, I've always thought that if worse came to worst, if life really got hard, I could always live aboard, at least temporarily, it would be like a shelter, I told myself. I could see myself living out my days in the cozy cabin of an Antares or a Merry Fisher tied up to a dock in some harbor. But that's not what I did.

No, said the judge. That's not what you did.

Otherwise I wouldn't be here, I said.

No, said the judge, otherwise you wouldn't be here.

It felt weird to hear him say that, like it was sarcastic, or, I don't know, like he was turning the knife in a wound in me, and he was opening it without my knowing if he was doing it for fun or if he was just following the straight line of facts, if the straight line of facts was also the sum of all the things left out, or abandoned, or unfinished, if the straight line of facts was like a series of wrong answers to a big questionnaire.

In any case, I was in a good position to see Antoine Lazenec coming, with those pointy shoes of his. I don't know why, but I've never liked shoes with pointed toes, those Italian shoes that look polished even in the rain. And it's not like I was in the habit of starting with people's feet when I met them, but I was cutting the estate lawn and had my head down watching the mower move across the grass and not hearing much of anything around me. So the first thing I saw were his leather shoes on the path, and also because they were so black and shiny against the white gravel. So I looked up and saw a guy, not too tall and almost bald, wearing a black jacket with his shirt collar open like a Parisian. He was looking at me without really smiling, waiting for me to turn the mower off. When I cut the motor there was this sudden silence, and he just said, Is all this for sale?

I could hear him jingling keys in his pocket while he looked at the château, as if he had taken in the whole property at a glance, the five acres facing the sea and the old freestone building, in a single "all this," and was already appropriating it. I could see his ivory or cream-colored sports car behind him gleaming in the sun, because it was sunny that day—see, we do get sunshine around here sometimes.

Yes, it's for sale, I said. The château and the five acres of the grounds, it's all for sale.

There was a silence as the two of us stood in the shade of the building, me wiping the damp grass off the mower blade, him standing in the calm weather—there was hardly any wind that day—with his hands still in his pockets.

I could tell he was expecting something, so I said: Are you here to see the place?

That's right.

Do you want me to open it for you?

No, he said. I'm waiting for someone.

So there we were again, between two awkward sentences, one keeping an eye out for whatever he was expecting, the other looking at the orchard descending toward the water, the first apples already bending the branches, and Erwan playing with his soccer ball under the trees a little farther down. So maybe because neither of us knew where to look, and maybe because I didn't dare start the mower again, because at times like that you try to find something to hang your thoughts on, like a coatrack, anyway he started the conversation again, and said: Is that your son?

Yes, I said.

He seems to like soccer.

Yes.

Are you a soccer fan?

Pretty much.

What's your son's name?

Erwan.

How old is he?

Ten, going on eleven.

He was starting to look impatient, glancing toward the road to see if anyone was coming, with his hand still in his pocket, jingling his keys. At that point, I didn't think he was more likely to buy the place than anyone else, because I'd already seen a few of them coming, guys in suits with wallets probably bigger than their hearts, but when I showed them inside and we went into the big medieval hall and they saw how dilapidated it was, most of them backed off. As time went on, I wound up thinking I'd be able to string this job along forever, showing the château like a tour guide to people who would never buy it, and living there in the groundskeeper's house until the end of my days.

The place was maybe five hundred square feet, set back from the sea where it blew pretty hard sometimes, but it had thick stone walls, and the living room and two bedrooms were enough for the pair of us, I mean Erwan and me, even if it didn't get much light and dormice nested in the fiberglass, and even if the pine needles kept the grass from growing in the shade of the evergreens' branches; there've always been evergreens here. In winter the pines keep what little light there is from reaching the living room or the kitchen, at least other than filtered through the trees, as if they were dumping their load of green and brown needles right onto the kitchen floor tiles, but it never bothered me. I'm like that too, like an old evergreen.

Erwan sometimes says that now, that I'm an old tree unable to move, probably with the same dry, almost poisonous old bark, which has been putting down roots under the walls all this time. Erwan grew up so fast these last years, amazing how they change, our kids, we barely blink and suddenly they seem as old as us.

How old is he now? asked the judge.

Seventeen. I should have said *only* seventeen, as if the past six years had lasted as long as twenty. Now that those years have passed, and especially all those visits I paid my son each week, with him behind the glass in the visitors' room, I see the whole story differently, you understand. But that day, on the estate with my mower tipped over and Erwan holding his ball, the day Antoine Lazenec showed up, how could we have foretold our future, Erwan's and mine, written on his skin? I don't usually judge people at first glance, so for me he was just an ordinary visitor, the kind we often got of a Saturday afternoon, taking advantage of the fact that the place was open to come have a look.

It was only when we heard hurried footsteps on the gravel, and I saw Martial Le Goff coming up the path, that I realized this wasn't usual, because the mayor didn't usually come to greet a possible buyer, much less apologize for being late, the way he did, out of breath from having run, as if he were afraid of missing the start, all sweaty because of his weight. Le Goff was pretty fat, the way you'd imagine a village mayor to be fat, with the high color you'd imagine a mayor's face to have, kind of like my own high color, and for good reason. We probably did the same amount of drinking over our lifetimes, and often together. We knew each other well, all those years on the town council voting for projects together, all those lobster pots we hauled up together in his little fishing boat, when you could spend the whole day on the water doing nothing but watching the shadows of fishes under the surface.

And we were neighbors. From my bedroom, I could make out Catherine in the distance peeling her vegetables at the sink, with Le Goff in the foreground having a whiskey while he watched the news on TV.

And we had the same first name. It's funny, we're both called Martial. So besides being on the same side politically, that brought us together. Le Goff and I were close, is what I'm saying.

And he was a good mayor. He was a good mayor for the whole peninsula, once. But it's been a long time since Le Goff was a mayor, or even a man, God rest his soul. But that was sure to happen too, I told the judge, at least one person would wind up like that. A suicide.

The judge didn't react. All the time I was talking, shooting sentences into the air like arrows, looking to see where they would land, what file they would hit or bounce off of and spread across his desk like so many future tales, he didn't react, no sir. And yet the echo of the bullet from Le Goff's hunting rifle was still ringing through the whole town, without the reasons for what he'd done being brought to light, or rather without anyone wanting to. The local reporters just made a few cautious suggestions stuck under vague headlines like "The Peninsula Suicide" or "A Mayor's Strange Death," hinting at drinking or marriage problems. But that wasn't it, I said. Martial didn't have a marriage problem. If anyone had a marriage problem, I told the judge, the guy found sprawled on the ground some morning would have been me.

He didn't react to that, either. His face was getting harder and harder to read. He was letting me talk my head off any which way, a thousand thoughts crowding into a funnel whose inner laws of selection maybe he was trying to understand.

Anyway, Le Goff was still alive and very much the mayor on that Saturday when Lazenec and I saw him coming up the road, hustling as best he could along the gravel path, twice apologizing for being late while mopping his face with his silk handkerchief. I could tell the two of them knew each other well, at least to judge by their friendly gestures and the way they used each other's first names—Martial for one, Antoine for the other.

Did you two introduce yourselves? asked Le Goff.

No, I said, not really.

So after a moment the guy, the one I sometimes call the cowboy, finally looked me in the eye, put a fairly firm hand in mine, and said, Lazenec. That was it. He didn't say a thing about himself, as if that statement alone was enough to put his name in lights. Except that I'd never heard that particular name, much less known I was supposed to greet him like the messiah, at least for all the reasons that Le Goff would explain later, after Lazenec had left. You have to tell me what's going on, I told him then.

Yes, you have to tell me what's going on, I said when Lazenec had left after touring the estate, going through all the rooms without paying much attention to anything, it was as if he was showing us around, with him leading the way through the rooms and hallways. I remember that when he looked out the upstairs windows, he said, There's potential here, several times. You were right, Le Goff, there's potential. Looking at the land sloping gently to the sea, with the pine trees lined up in a sort of royal path to the water, he said he liked it very much. And he repeated that word, "potential."

Standing there at the old oak windows with his back to us, it was as though he had taken in the sky, the view of the channel, and the whitish city stepping down like a staircase, already taken all that in at a glance. Even now, he was trapping Le Goff's name as he talked. I wouldn't say I disliked him that day, that's not the right word, and even if something dark had been written on the windowpane, even with invisible ink, it would have been noticeable. I'm not one to shine spotlights from the recent past to illuminate the present, and I know very well that there's no compass come up from the bottom of the sea to show us the way. Often it's just the opposite: The present is what shines its light into the great depths of the sea.

As I think back on it, you know what strikes me the most about that visit? His ordinariness. That's right, ordinariness. The kind of guy you see in the street carrying a briefcase and maybe it's full of banknotes or kilos of cocaine, but what you think is, just insurance policies or frozen-food catalogs. Except maybe for his sports car, the likes of which we don't often see around here. It was a Porsche, to be exact, and even then I wouldn't have been able to tell, except that Erwan was there. Erwan came along on the whole tour, and later, when Lazenec drove off in a cloud of white dust, Erwan said, It's a Porsche, a 911. And, all of ten years old, he added, Is he going to buy the château?

So I looked at Le Goff and repeated what Erwan said: Is it true, he's going to buy the château?

Le Goff looked at me in turn, opened his eyes wider than usual, and said, Kermeur, don't you read the papers?

I could have answered that yes, usually I did, only sometimes I felt a little tired...In fact I hadn't bought the newspaper that morning. So Le Goff pulled that day's paper from his back pocket and unfolded it under my eyes. It had a huge headline saying something like "Big Plans for the Peninsula," and underneath it a photo of a balding guy with his shirt collar open, so I knew right away who it was, not to mention what he had in mind, because next to it was an interview that talked about all the plans in question. So I looked over the whole page as if I were already searching for the answer to a puzzle, and I came across words printed bigger than the rest that kind of exploded in my head, sentences with strange expressions like "real estate complex," "rental investment," "residential estate," and then off to one side lower down, like a kind of feverish conclusion that the reporter felt was worth stressing with an exclamation point: "a seaside resort!"

Imagine that, I told the judge, a seaside resort here on Brest Bay! And I continued reading the article line by line, with its big sentences like all the region lacked was the faith and courage to face the future, there was undeveloped potential here, it said, for generations we've been sitting on a gold mine covered by cabbages and artichokes, a new era of tourism and development was dawning, it was time to prepare to enter the new millennium, so that by the end of the article you'd think a kind of archangel had come down from big-city heaven to deck our consciences with flowers. First to weed them properly, our consciences, then plant seeds in our brains in the hopes of growing a boulevard, or even better, five-story buildings all glass and exotic woods with solariums, glass elevators, and heated swimming pools. But the expression that echoed in my skull wasn't "building" or "solarium." It was "seaside resort."

It's not as if we aren't used to this, having some crank appear from time to time and look down his nose at those of us who live here, saying we didn't how to make the most of our landscape, our miles of coastline without a hotel-restaurant or campground worthy of the name, or upscale apartments to enjoy the view, that beautiful light that hits the rocks in the late afternoon, the calm of the ferns that seem to absorb all the wind's pain…I could talk these places up too, and I love them more than any little speculator in the world ever could. The fog that comes and goes under the pale sun. The leaves of the trees when the storms move off.

But you don't live with things by shouting their praises in newspaper columns.

There on the château grounds, with the Porsche long gone, I took the time to read the whole article. And I told Le Goff that it was unbelievable, just nuts, that I should be the last person to learn about this.

Said the mayor: Kermeur, old man, we haven't seen much of you recently.

I remember trying to understand what the word "recently" implied. True, I'd kept pretty much to myself these last days, watching too much television or something, hoeing my flower beds next to the stone walls without bothering to look at the road or the town, or anything that was happening behind my back, as it were. After all, I'm nearly fifty, so digging my garden and looking after a son seemed like more than enough.

You're probably right, I told Martial as I handed his paper back, I've kept to myself too much these last days.

As he folded the paper and put it in his back pocket, he said: Kermeur, heaven itself sent us this guy.

Speaking of heaven, we felt blessed when what began as a persistent rumor going around town became an announcement of our whole future delivered with pomp and circumstance in the mayoralty's banquet hall. But you shouldn't imagine a huge hall like they have in big cities, with crystal chandeliers and glass alcoves with happy couples getting married. Ours is just a room that's a little bigger than the others, a little brighter, too, with a shinier floor that seems to catch the sun at eleven o'clock. I don't know why, but I've always especially liked the sunshine that pours in at eleven o'clock on holidays—if that's what you would call the day Le Goff invited us in to show off the scale model of the project, with the architects and of course Lazenec in the front row. It felt like a kind of miniature inauguration, with five hundred glasses already lined up on paper tablecloths as if they were part of the ceremony, if "ceremony" is the right word. In any case, it was something to see all of us peninsula people gathered in the hundreds, like we were involved. It really struck me.

The model was still covered by a red felt drape that Le Goff would pull off when he finished his speech, in the proudest and most majestic gesture of his whole tenure. And what a speech it was, the microphone squealing half the time and him saying that after the tough final years of the century someone had at last dared to cut through the prevailing grayness and that we could thank—you'll never guess the word he said next: heaven—heaven for bringing us Antoine Lazenec, who needed no introduction, he'd been seen in all the places where he needed to be seen...No, he didn't say it like that, more like who had been seen everywhere these last months, in the local newspaper, in the soccer stadium, at that charity banquet organized by the club with the animal name. It seemed he suddenly had the gift of being everywhere at once, so that people had long since put a name to his face, the same face that was getting fatter under our very eyes from all his business meetings in fancy restaurants. Those of us shipyard workers and longshoremen who lived on the peninsula were cheerfully watching him trample our flower beds, those same flower beds we'd been tending our whole lives without even knowing he existed, and which certainly didn't need any fertilizer to make things grow faster.

Lazenec behaved like a pioneer discovering a new land. We were like naïve, bewildered Indians, unsure whether to shoot a poisoned arrow or welcome him with open arms, but it certainly seemed we chose the second option. When he took the microphone from Le Goff that morning in the mayoralty hall, it was as if a spotlight suddenly lit up his face and the whole village held its collective breath, waiting for the word from a developer.

He took the microphone and started by thanking Le Goff and, of course, the architects, who were standing like silent mummies in black jackets, then all the local notables who had opened their doors to him—but the doors to what, Your Honor?—without forgetting anyone, not a banker or a mayor or a vice president, all those people he apparently met in back rooms around the city, businessmen of every stripe who were already rubbing their hands at having signed the biggest contract of the decade, and at that moment not sorry to have given up their Sundays to play yet another round of golf or to have yet another drink in some nightclub where business was being done. I'm not telling you anything you don't know, since as an examining magistrate you're supposed to take a panoramic view of the city's affairs. Not at the outset, of course, but gradually, day by day, because of your investigations—and I don't know anything about that because I'm not a judge—but it must be like soaring over the buildings in a hot-air balloon, where each new clue adds more hot air and you rise a little more, so eventually you're high above the city and the things that connect the city to itself, and you can start to see new streets, not just commercial streets crowded with people on Saturday afternoon, and

not the windy side streets but new streets, streets that are—
how can I put this?—more aerial, more invisible, streets that
only exist on drawings, virtual avenues cutting across the
map, from the mayor's office to the exhibition hall, from the
exhibition hall to the Banque de l'Ouest, from the harbor to
the courthouse, except that instead of people moving along
those streets and avenues that are like cracks sharper than
architects' lines, there's especially—what?—secrets being
told, secrets and money, of course, and also girls, of course,
well, not really girls but, let's say, sex, so that in the end, if
you add it all up, the secrets, the money, and the sex, you
have everything. Everything, see.

After that, a kind of silence fell between the judge and
me, as if we felt like taking a moment to think of a way to
hold it all back—not the events themselves, it was much too
late for that, but our feeling of disgust under the gray sky
outside the window.

It's true that people like me don't get out enough to learn
all the city's ways, I continued. Yet how far are we from the
city? Not even eight miles. But there's the bridge, and maybe
a bridge is supposed to bring people together, but it's still
a bridge, with the ocean under it coming up every twelve
hours. We live on a peninsula, remember, so for guys like Le
Goff and me, there'll always been an ocean underneath that
cuts us off from certain places.

You should have seen it when Le Goff pulled away the
red drape and we all came close: There in a glass box at least

six by nine feet, lit from above by two spotlights, was a scale model of the whole peninsula, with its fields and cliffs, its farms and houses, the church and the village square.

Our peninsula, I thought.

And we applauded. I'm not sure what we were applauding—the moment, the scale model, maybe Lazenec himself. We crowded around the model, leaning close and admiring the level of detail, each one looking for their own house on the plastic streets. It was like an electric-train layout in the window of a toy store.

Except that instead of an electric train, the thing that right away caught people's eye was the five future buildings facing the sea and surrounded by luminous grounds, taller than everything else and putting the château in the shade. They had gone so far as to put tiny people on the terraces overlooking the ocean—only it wasn't really the ocean but a sheet of blue plastic that represented it—and a long beach with real sand dug from the actual project site. Even the little plastic trees in front of the buildings seemed to have grown during the night. At one point or other that morning, we all lived inside that glass box, which no rain or dust would ever enter. We were drawn to the future like a magnet.

True, it was just a model, but the sun already seemed to be reflected in its windows and aluminum tracks. Because of the aerial view we suddenly had, we were coming to grips with the coast in this absurd and millennial encounter, seeing it reduced to such a small scale for the first time, and we emerged triumphant. I remember seeing people at the door picking up the prospectus with *Les Grands Sables, a Future for the Peninsula* in big type and Lazenec's picture on the back like a flyer in a municipal election.

But if France were one big casino table, everyone here knows the odds are a hundred to one against you, I told the judge. You'd have to be a gambler, a real gambler, to brave the local economy's age-old rules and win over people long resigned to failure and weary of the mirages and promises they were so often sold in the local newspapers, without any of them even seeing a start. You had to believe that times were changing, if you know what I mean, that something more urban was reaching out to us, and that seemed to be the direction things were headed.

Maybe that's the way it is everywhere now, I told the judge, in all those places that were once villages but you can't really call towns. All those places where the plains have been paved over and the weeds take revenge by cracking the schoolyard playgrounds. Like everywhere else, it was always a head-scratcher for us when we had to put up new signs marking our city limits. As if we were never sure what would justify the boundaries, or what would move them again: vacant lots or farmer's fields taken over one by one by some visionary developer, or someone who thought he was a visionary and finally became one because sometimes it was enough just to submit some sort of construction plan to the town council, and before you knew it, there was yet another scale model and yet more land being taken over.

I know what I'm talking about, because I was on the town council too. I would've done better to stay on it, now that I know what decision we should have taken. But then again, I probably would've done like everyone else. The left and the right pretty much split the council seats between them, and it was all the more comfortable for me because I was with the majority. In those years, if you were a Socialist, you were almost always in the majority. Heck, the whole country was Socialist. We'd already won the national elections twice in a row.

You were too young then, but you have to realize what 1981 was for us, I told the judge. A year is a funny thing. It takes on a certain hue, and faces emerge from it even thirty years later. And especially 1981, the year Erwan was born.

We were at the clinic when President Mitterrand's face was on the TV, as a matter of fact. That was something you'd never forget, the presidential vote count that seemed to be helping my wife give birth, so that the next day—that's right, the very next day—we had a son, and it's as if the cars honking in the streets all night long had been as much for Erwan's arrival as for the new president. In the years since then, that honking has died away somewhere deep in our brains, as if it had shrunk, and in my head, anyway, the events of my times have shriveled. Maybe that phrase doesn't exist, but I want to invent it in this case, now that I'm finally talking about the twenty or thirty years that have gone through us, or past us. I'm not sure how to say that either, but there was a time when we actually felt we had some wind at our backs. It's not that the sea is flat calm today; maybe it's just that I don't have the ears to hear that wind blowing anymore. That's what Erwan thinks. He's often said that I'm now too tired to hear the wind anywhere except at sea, that I've aged faster than is normal, whereas for him, that kind of wind still blows very loudly in him, as loudly as the music he used to listen to in his bedroom. I would really like it if music was still playing in his bedroom today.

But I was tired, and besides, Erwan was getting older and I felt it would be good to have more time to take care of him, so I didn't run for reelection. That was just as well for me, don't you know, since it was then that things fell apart with France. Erwan's mother was named France, see. Well, she's still named France, but I don't often call her by her first name anymore, let's say. She thinks that everything that's happened since is my fault. Maybe she's right. I told her that one day: Maybe you're right, everything that's happened is probably my fault.

In any case it was just when I quit the town council that she began to feel I was spending too much time around the house. It's better for men to be busy all the time, otherwise we become a pain in the neck, or at least women soon feel we're a pain in the neck, standing in front of the fireplace smoking instead of maybe washing the windows or vacuuming, whereas if we come home from town council meetings at midnight every night, they find that normal. I don't think she ever understood that, the empty hours I spent in the living room with the *Télégramme*—assuming I'd managed to go buy the paper—when I'd lie on the sofa and read it cover to cover. So it was better for her to leave, since in the last years I've at least doubled the time I spend on the sofa or in front of the mirror over the fireplace, the mirror whose glass is so cracked and cloudy I can hardly see the reflection of my face, just shadows and shapes in front of it. I insisted that she leave me that mirror. It's not that I don't want to see what it shows, I told the judge, but I just can't help it, the longer I look at it, the more I feel like I'm trapped inside the glass, my brain caught in the mist that you might mistake for any other winter morning with the sun trying to shine through it, except it's paler or washed out by the mirror's opaque texture. And the closer you get, the more you're caught by the cloudy cracks in the glass. At times I get lost there, in the fog of the mirror, in my wavy reflection. Sometimes I'm happy to get lost there, but sometimes I get angry, I told the judge, angry at the fog.

I would have preferred if you had stayed angry at the fog, and only the fog, he said.

Yes, that's for sure, I said.

So as not to have to meet his gaze for too long, I dropped my eyes to the bound penal code standing upright on the desk. I didn't dare look even a millimeter farther up the cover, as if it were a wall too high that you'd have to climb just to see what was on the other side. On the other side of the laws, provisions, and paragraphs, he wasn't seeing crimes and spectacular crime scenes anymore but only convictions and sentences, so that the only thing to be read on the judge's face, which I didn't want to look at, was prison corridors I could imagine myself being led along in handcuffs with my head down, looking at the harbor through the cell windows upstairs, waiting for a visit by France. Which wasn't very likely to happen, I realized.

So there you have it, I told the judge. He fooled everybody. I'll say this: If we could just glimpse the demon lurking in people's hearts and see it instead of a smooth, smiling face, it would be obvious, wouldn't it?

Looking down at his desk, the judge leafed through his pile of accumulated paperwork, opening one folder after another. Finally he found a picture, glanced at it for a moment, and slid it toward me. It was a newspaper photograph taken that day with Lazenec and Le Goff and a few other suits in the frame. They were all standing in front of the scale model and smiling like children in a class photo.

Look at him, I said. Who does he look like? He looks like you or me.

You really don't expect the devil to look like Robert Mitchum, do you? he asked.

No, of course not, not Robert Mitchum. But you could certainly see a photo like that in some movie, pinned to the bulletin board in a police station, with the faces outlined in black felt-tip pen. But that's easy for me to say now. On that morning, as the glasses of white wine started going around, the very word "developer" seemed to sparkle like sunlight.

Le Goff was strutting in front of the scale model and I remember his voice when he said to me, It looks like the real thing, doesn't it? He patted me on the shoulder, trying to retrieve some friendly thing that was slipping away from us, something that we were now in danger of losing as he moved through the crowd with the same energy as when he celebrated his victory in the election. Standing right next to the model, he'd suddenly justified his two terms as mayor in front of all the regional big shots who had bothered to come, the people who would give their speeches in turn, either hailing the future or cracking jokes about the weather. That day I realized they really had decided to locate their seaside resort here, despite the fog over the shipyards that never lifts and the wind that blows two days out of three. But each of them was careful not to use the actual expression "seaside resort." They used more modest phrases instead, like "apartment block" or "complex," and one they especially liked, "real estate complex."

All in all, it felt like a wedding, I told the judge. Even the women had gotten dressed up. The children were running this way and that, except Erwan. He stayed right next to me the whole time. I remember that very well because it was the day before he turned eleven, and that afternoon I had promised we would go to town to buy him a new fishing rod for his birthday. That's right, he was only eleven when this whole business started. His voice was still high, and he certainly wasn't thinking of piercing his nostrils. I sure can't pat him on the head the way I did that day, and he sure isn't about to look up at me the way he did and ask, Are we going to buy an apartment in the model?

And I remember smiling as I answered: I don't think so, Erwan. This project isn't for us.

Le Goff was standing nearby and he overheard, so he leaned down to Erwan and said: Your father isn't the kind of guy to go into real estate, you know.

I smiled without answering, and for good reason. I didn't have anything to say and I didn't know any more about all this than a ten-year-old kid, any more than Erwan did, who was looking at the model like a toy he might've enjoyed building. And if I could've understood that morning how Erwan's mind would soon be working, if I could've understood that at ten or eleven you can already be so open to a father's affairs, for sure I would've made him go play hide-and-seek or something with the other children.

Maybe Le Goff found me a little distant, or worried, I don't know, but he felt he had to add something like: Don't worry, Martial, for us, you'll always be our groundskeeper.

As a matter of fact, I wanted to talk to you about that, I said. It bothers me a little to ask you this, but Erwan and I are happy where we are, so do you think I'll be able to go on living there among all these big projects?

Lazenec himself was standing nearby. All that time he was never more than ten feet from the model, as if he always had to cast his shadow over the buildings and the green spaces, and over the tiny people on the rooftop terraces. You would've thought Lazenec was like a rain cloud hiding the sun from them. Le Goff waved to him, and he came over to us.

Monsieur Lazenec, Le Goff said, you know Kermeur, don't you?

Of course, he answered.

About his house at the entrance of the estate, he'd really like to know if—

Before Le Goff could finish his sentence, Lazenec said: Oh yes, that's right, you mentioned that little easement problem.

Easement? I said. What's an easement?

Le Goff was the one I turned to at that moment. He couldn't have expected to hear a word like that used but he wasn't about to contradict Lazenec, so he stammered, casting about with "that is to say," and "in the end," and "you see," so that I eventually understood that "easement" didn't mean that I was being eased out. But it did mean something like a pebble in your shoe.

So the guy, the cowboy, who kept his hand in his pocket, eventually looked me in the eye and said: Yes, of course, we'll have to discuss that. And then, to change the subject—I don't know if it was instinctive or not—he looked at Erwan and asked if he liked soccer. You understand, I told the judge, he didn't say, "Don't worry" or "We'll work something out." No, he'd noticed a ten-year-old boy with a red-and-white fan scarf around his neck and asked him if he liked soccer. Erwan looked at me as if he were hesitant to answer, because that's the way he was, Erwan, kind of shy.

Imagining Erwan as shy might strike you as odd today, but I assure you that if he could have hidden in my pocket at that moment he would've done it, to the point that I was the one who answered, I was the one who said, Of course, yes, he loves soccer.

I didn't bother telling Lazenec that we were season ticket holders at the stadium, that we wouldn't miss a game for anything in the world, seated up there in the fan section with the cheering and the cold and the air horns blasting in the night. I didn't bother telling him that we had already seen him, Lazenec, in his glass luxury box on the heated levels reserved for local big shots. There he was with his collar open as usual, chatting with the club president or the owner of some supermarket whose name was written in big letters on the players' jerseys, while we pulled our anoraks up to our necks in the north grandstand wind. I didn't bother saying that the first time we had seen him was that same afternoon when he first visited the château. Sitting in the north grandstand, we recognized Lazenec, or at least Erwan did. He tugged on my arm and pointed to him, up there in a box, saying, That's the guy from this afternoon, and so I looked at the stadium boxes. And then I better understood why Le Goff followed him around like his shadow. What I should've thought that evening, and what I've learned to think since, is that it's never a good sign to run into twice in the same day a guy you didn't know the day before.

There in the mayoralty hall, as the crowd began to thin out and people left with their prospectus and their seaside-resort dreams, Lazenec bent down to Erwan like an old family friend and said: I'll take you next time, if you like. I've got seats in the central skybox, and the players come to see us after the game.

So try to imagine, I told the judge, just try to imagine the light shining on the harbor the day he drove up in his sports car and took Erwan to the Brest Stadium's manager's box. At the far end of the stadium that night, huddled against the wind, I saw my own son nice and warm behind glass, with hostesses bringing him orange juice on a tray, with Lazenec next to him, and the two of them sitting beside the club president. Try to imagine that at the end of the game, instead of his going home with the rest of us—a little drunk by now—the players came to the box and gave Erwan a jersey they had all signed. Open his closets today and you'll find at least a dozen of those shirts. He even has a jersey signed by Juan Cesar. Can you imagine?

I don't know anything about soccer, said the judge.

Yeah, of course, but it's just to say that this whole story—

This whole story is mainly your story, said the judge.

Yes, of course. It's mine. But let me tell it the way I want to, let it be like a wild river that sometimes overflows its banks, because I don't have a lot of knowledge and laws like you do, and because in telling it my way, I don't know, it eases my heart a little, as if I were floating, or something like that, maybe as if nothing had happened or even, and maybe especially, as if as long as I'm talking, as long as I haven't finished talking, then right here, right in front of you, nothing can happen to me, as if for once I could suspend the cascade of catastrophes that has been crashing down on me nonstop, like dominoes I took years to patiently set up that were collapsing without warning, one after another.

Anyway, it wasn't long after that before we started seeing guys in flannel suits roaming the subdivision streets and sitting down at living-room coffee tables to unfold their plans and recite their memorized sales pitches, eager to close on a two-bedroom apartment with an ocean view, while maybe trying to hide their contempt for the place mats on the dining-room tables because they looked too much like the ones their parents used, whereas they were what? Thirty or thirty-five years old at the most, with businessmen's attaché cases, pink shirts, and black patent leather shoes, trying hard not to look like their parents, who were of a generation with some pretty good years behind them, except that the stucco façades built twenty years earlier were showing signs of wear, and were eroding faster than the savings balance in their bank books. I know what I'm talking about. I used to have one of those bank books, too.

Did they know that my account recently got the four hundred thousand francs from the Arsenal? No, not the guys in the flannel suits. The moment I saw them making their way up the next street over, looking for all the world like Jehovah's Witnesses come to talk about the Bible, I'd often duck down under my window while they rang my doorbell. When they stepped into houses, their eyes had that same strange light as if they were bringing the word of God. Except that instead of God, they had Lazenec.

That's right, Lazenec. You would've thought he'd planned it all since forever, as if when he was fifteen or seventeen he'd written everything out in a kind of diary covering the next thirty years, and it was sufficiently fixed in his mind that he didn't doubt for a minute that he would get what he was after. On that score, experience has taught me that everything depends on the chisel you use to carve the marble that serves as our brain. And it all depends on how hard you press the chisel. In his case, I'm sure he didn't hesitate to press very hard inside himself and never strayed from the mental groove that would get him where he wanted to go and sweep us along with him.

Yes, sweep us along, I often thought as I looked at the estate's five acres spread out under my window, which were beginning to reshape themselves vertically in our heads—and only in our heads—by dint of words like "duplex," like "solarium," like "fitness." One day a billboard was put up at the estate entrance that had this written on it, I swear: "Coming Soon: The Saint-Tropez of Finistère."

Today I don't know if it hurt me to have gotten what you might call special treatment, I mean not having to deal with the little commercial agents paid on commission, every word out of their mouths like a barnacle stuck to a whale. In a way, I had the strange privilege of talking to God Almighty instead of his saints, because Lazenec came onto his property so often. That was another thing I had to get used to, the fact that the château, something that had belonged to everyone for three centuries, was now the property of just one person who came every week, or almost, accompanied by swarms of guys in neckties, for soil studies, or the land registry, or what have you. As time went on, he started calling me by my first name, and later still to greet me with a hug and kiss.

You heard that right, I told the judge, he started kissing me. You've been in the South of France, so you must've seen plenty of guys who kiss everyone in sight while holding a knife in their other hand. We like to think that just happens down south and not here in the north, of course. But even if you know full well that there's nothing reassuring about a guy who hugs you so warmly, even if you have that stamped in black on white deep in your skull, when it happens to you, it's not the same.

Maybe Le Goff was right, maybe I had been too isolated recently. The first person to break through that loneliness, you don't give a damn who it is, so long as you take it all in and it fits you like the piece of the puzzle that you could have cut out on purpose to perfectly fit your soul. That's just the way it is. And that's maybe the main thing I've learned in these last ten years: You always wind up loving the ones who love you.

This isn't something I would've told you back in the day, but I've had time to think recently, time to look at the scratches in the mirror above the fireplace and to meditate on the color of each hour, I've had time to realize that I was like rich compost at the best planting season, where anything would've taken root in me and opened and flowered like at a garden show, to the point that I think Lazenec and I became friends, as it were.

But I hope you heard when I said "as it were," because in reality you'd have to stick in a big silence, open an enormous parentheses that you would leave empty, just filled with the stink that was starting to hang over the harbor. I swear I've gone over the process a hundred times in my head, I told the judge, trying to see just when things between him and me went off the rails, and after six years, here in front of you, all I've come up with is to add "as it were." Because it's a problem that can't be solved, when somebody like him approaches you, to know exactly when the sting happened.

I'm pretty sure I then looked up at the ceiling, which seemed to serve as our sky, over our entire world, the judge's and mine, contained in that office.

Just the same, there must have been a beginning for you, he said.

Yes, that's true, there was a beginning for me, or I should say a flaw in me. There was a flaw in me and he blew into it like the wind, because he was always blowing as hard as the wind, always working his way into any crack or fissure of the false front I had put up and was trying to pretend was brick, but the fact is, I'm not made of granite. Otherwise how can you explain the fact that I wound up in the passenger seat next to him in his Porsche one day, driving on the highway along the sea to go have a beer in the harbor, the only reason being to talk about fishing and especially boats, since he'd just bought a boat, the very kind that I'd been thinking of buying with the money from the Arsenal. What a coincidence, I'd once said to Lazenec, because I was thinking of getting the very same model.

How could I have known that right there, my saying that one thing among a thousand other things I'd said, with him standing at my front door about to leave, as usual, when we were talking about fishing, as usual, that I had the misfortune to tell him that I too was thinking of buying a thirty-foot Merry Fisher? How could I have known that with just those few words, I could bring myself so much bad luck?

Actually, that wasn't the bad luck. The bad luck was that I hinted I had the money for it, that I could do it. And Lazenec wondered how a guy like me could afford to buy himself a Merry Fisher.

Right away I saw that he was thinking something like that, from the way he made his face blank, freezing it a little to hide his surprise. And then he asked a question in his roundabout way, with just the right touch of condescension: Secondhand?

No, new, I said. I plan to buy a new one.

He just stood there without saying anything, except maybe his shoulders twitched a little. What would you have done if you were in my shoes then? I asked the judge, if you're looking at a blank face that seems to be expecting you to come up with explanations? Because that's what happened. I imagined he was thinking things and I imagined I had to answer, that I had to justify myself to him, how it was possible that I, Martial Kermeur, a shipwright at the Brest Arsenal, could afford to buy himself a brand-new thirty-foot Merry Fisher? So what do you suppose I did? I told him the whole story. About my being laid off, about all the guys in the region getting their bonuses, about my four hundred thousand francs in compensation.

I could tell that this interested him a lot, and do you know how I sensed that? Because it was the only time I ever spoke for more than a minute at a time without him saying anything. He didn't say a word, just listened to me without asking any questions, I don't know, maybe like when you go see a psychologist for the first time and you tell him your story, and he lets you roll it out like a red carpet under your feet. But standing there at my front door, how could I have known that I was rolling out the red carpet for Lazenec?

Still, he left that evening like nothing was out of the ordinary. He got behind the wheel of his Porsche as usual and left. And do you suppose he approached me directly after that? I asked the judge. Of course he didn't. Besides, do you think I would've given in so easily? No way. Quite the contrary. He let as much time as necessary go by after that, letting the days pile up and cover the things I'd said so I'd forget them and, worse, forget that there might be a connection between them. It's only now that I'm thinking about all this in front of you, that I'm gathering my memories and lifting the veil he was able to lay down and stretch far enough to scatter the pieces underneath it.

We were in front of the château about a month later, talking fishing and boats again, and he mentioned the Merry Fisher he'd just bought, and I didn't see the connection he'd made in his head. For him this was a good excuse to act friendly, and that's what he wanted, to act friendly, friendly enough so that we'd eventually wind up standing in front of his new boat.

And that's what happened. He drove me to the harbor in his Porsche. He put some awful music on the car radio and we crossed the bridge over the harbor. On Dock A of the marina we stood for a long time, arms folded, in front of a Merry Fisher 930, calmly chatting, yes calmly, because a dock in a harbor can calm the whole world, especially if you go there right at six in the evening when the sun is setting over the channel and flashes its great cutting light before disappearing.

We could see our château bathed in all that light, standing above the calm water on the other side of the harbor, standing there as if for all time.

From here, you'd think it was a real castle, I said.

That's true, he said. It's almost a shame to tear it down.

Tear it down? I asked.

While I was still digesting what he'd said, he was already walking toward the quay. I followed him, trying to say that I didn't understand, that on the scale model it seemed that the castle—

Yes, he said, but what can I say? The project is evolving. Besides, Kermeur, it'll be much more beautiful this way, you'll see.

And I followed him up the gangway without quite knowing what to think. But at moments like that, Lazenec was thinking for two, as we walked away from the boats' silent masts and went to sit on the terrace of the only bar open in the marina, which was like a mezzanine above the sea. And to be honest, when a guy like that invites you to have a beer, I told the judge, you never know if he's doing it just because he's alone that evening, or because he has something in mind, or maybe because he's proud of himself because you're the last person he would have thought to bring there, and he's feeling proud at condescending to you. Since then I've understood that a guy like that always wants to have his cake and eat it too, and for Lazenec, eating the cake meant being friendly toward me for a while. And I sort of went along with him in that friendship.

In the end, you and I are kind of similar, he said. We're like two estate managers, each in his own way.

I think I must've pursed my lips dubiously, to agree but also to not pick up on the point. He continued looking off in the distance, and you would've thought that just by looking he'd already erased the old building that served as our château, and I in turn could see it gently fading into the future, while he was saying that the advantage of the region was that the price per square foot was still affordable, and it was stable, and this was the sort of place where you couldn't lose money, in fact it was the opposite because thanks to investments like his the price per square foot would rise, not to mention the economic fabric of the peninsula. I listened to him make his speech, with that manner he had of acting as if he was just mentioning all these stories about real estate and a bright future to me, but they really didn't concern me, that is, he mentioned it with a kind of casualness. Notice his casualness, I told the judge. Here's a guy who's talking to you but could well not talk to you, and giving you the impression that everything he's saying is happening somewhere else, far away, without you, so by the time he's finished, if he's done everything right, all you want is to be part of it. Lazenec knows that, he knows that's the way it works.

Now I'm telling you this today as if I had all the clues in hand from the very beginning, but of course it wasn't like that at all, I was as blind as Saint Paul after he fell off his horse. And I couldn't tell you the way things followed one after another, the way the weather shifts into a string of rainy days. It was more like a fog bank moved in without our knowing when it started or what part of the road it covered. That evening I felt that everything was being enveloped in one slow movement, like a tightly spun cloth where you can't make out the weave, because of the way things he said were being laid down like sediment on the bottom of a river. So it was no accident when he spoke up, interrupting himself, to say: You know, Kermeur, I think I owe you an apology.

An apology? I said. Whatever for?

Because I haven't given you a chance to invest.

He said this as an offhand remark, maybe out of politeness, or at least I thought that he said it that way because there was already a bill on the table to pay for our beer, and I didn't yet know that a dozen guys like me had probably been drawn into the same scene, enjoying the same hours of friendship constructed for the occasion, and told not to miss out on a deal like this, a brand-new apartment with a view of the harbor.

It should be said that he never presented it as a place to live in. He talked about investment and return but never living, so it remained like lines drawn by an architect without any substance between them. In the two hours we spent there on the harbor in the cool of the late afternoon, I didn't hear a single word about living or dwelling. It was as if words like "functional" or "bright" or "modern" were only created to complete the expression "at maturity." I remember that I asked him: What exactly does "at maturity" mean? I'm not sure I understood his answer, but I remember that "at maturity" you could make a lot of money, something like a 10 to 12 percent annual return—and I'm not sure I quite understood that either—except that it meant a lot of extra money for the owner.

I would have wanted to add an adverb like "probably," "eventually," or "maybe" to each thing he said. Saying this today, I wouldn't be short of adverbs, but on that day I didn't have the time to see things that way, with adverbs, since I was bending under the weight of his accumulated data while he continued to talk generally, in other words to everyone else except me, and trying to make me out to be more independent than I was. This is something he understood perfectly that evening when he said, I'm not the person to tell you what you should do, Kermeur. You know how to steer your own ship.

And you can't imagine, I told the judge, that ten-foot waves rose like walls of water in that brain of mine at this sudden idea of steering my own ship, as if I were on that ship, lost in the middle of the ocean next to a huge liner bound for America. So because of that very feeling, under my skull, it was like a magic bullet fired from one side to the other and breaking all the windows. And at the same time as this ricocheting bullet was doing more damage than a stone tossed into a lake—at the same time, I'm saying—something in me was swelling with pride or, I don't know, sovereignty, something that was saying, Yes it's true you know how to steer your own ship, without realizing that Lazenec would soon be making himself at home in my pride, my resistance, and my free will, flopping down on a leather sofa he had upholstered himself.

We went on drinking our beers while we watched the sea under the setting sun. And we continued to talk about fishing and about his new life in the region, and this whole future opening up to the peninsula. He never stopped planting seeds in my brain, the way you broadcast seeds in a field, with the same ease where you know that not all of the seeds will take root, that some will rot on a stone or be eaten by birds, but it doesn't matter, because you scatter so many seeds that enough of them will grow into a uniform carpet of grass. Well, this was exactly the same thing, I told the judge.

From that moment on, it was as if the captain who was supposed to be living with me in my brain had abandoned the ship even before the wreck began. And maybe he was on some distant rock, his eyes wild, that captain who's lived inside me for more than fifty years without stumbling and had suddenly left and was watching from shore as the ship sank.

Thinking is a strange business, isn't it? It's not that it's so far from your brain to your lips, but sometimes it can seem like miles, that for a sentence to make the trip, it would be like crossing a war zone with a sack of stones on your shoulder, to the point where even a thought that seems firm and solid, considered and reconsidered a hundred times, chooses to take shelter behind some sandbags. What I'm trying to say is that in the following days, instead of clearly saying "No," which was going on inside me, instead of letting myself be led back to my groundskeeper job with the friendly self-regard I carried in my heart, instead of that, with the voice of a ghost who can hear himself, I picked up the phone one evening and said, "Lazenec?" And then I said, "Why not?" And I said, "When do I sign?"

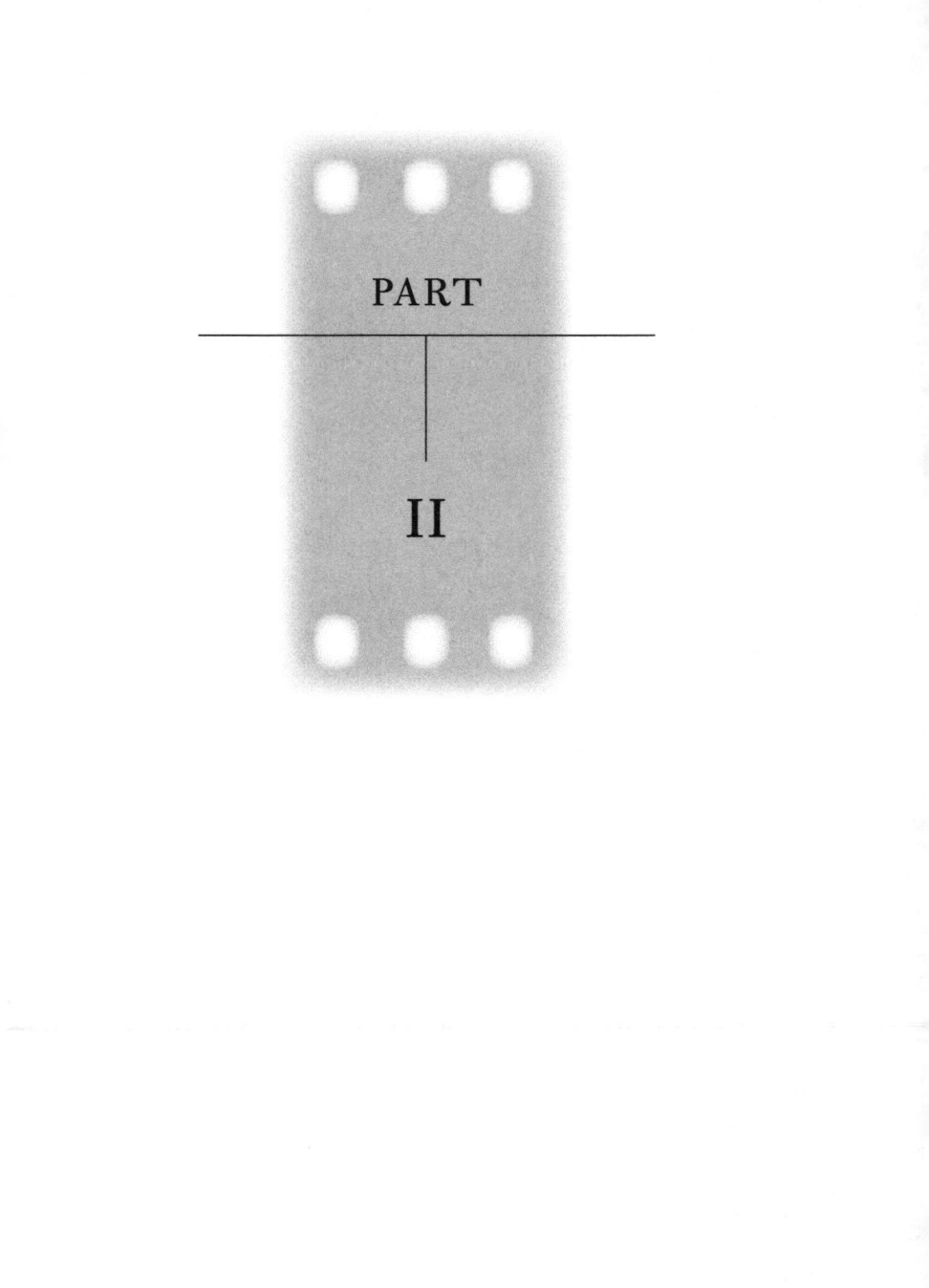

PART

II

The judge was on his feet now, looking out the window. Backlit that way, with his hands behind his back, he looked maybe twenty years older, in the way that people's ages can vary from one minute to the next with a frown or a change of the light. So it didn't help when he spun around, with his backlit face now dark and only his voice coming out of the shadows, saying: For heaven's sake, Kermeur, what were you thinking? He slammed his fist on his desk, almost knocking off the documents piled there.

I think it scared me, that a guy who's supposed to stand for the calm and coldness of the law should get so angry and seem so emotional. It actually did scare me, and I kept my eyes fixed on the ground, letting his question sink into the strips of the old parquet floor creaking under our feet. I don't remember what happened just then. I don't remember if he repeated his question two or three times or if it was just pounding like a drum inside me. What I do know is that all I could think to say was, Can I step outside for a minute?

The judge looked at his watch and then the wall clock hanging behind me, as if to make sure that they were properly synchronized. Then, without answering, he walked around his desk, opened the door, and called the cop outside to escort me down the hall. At that moment, maybe I should've run and let myself be shot down on the courthouse steps, but maybe he also knew I wouldn't do that.

His question continued to echo in the faded hallway and was still echoing as the flow of urine streamed into the toilet bowl. His voice echoed off the tile squares of the toilet wall: For heaven's sake, Kermeur, what were you thinking? And it seemed to ravage me like insecticide sprayed on a ladybug, as if in that instant my own body was just that, a ladybug being blown over. Then I walked back the way I'd come, to that same badly painted office, with the judge on the other side of his penal code, as it were. In the meantime, he had sat back down and erased the anger flowing through his body, as if the leather of his armchair diffused a kind of soothing balm around him. I couldn't tell whether he was annoyed at me for having signed or only angry at himself for having gotten carried away—carried away over a guy he would soon be leading to the gates of a prison.

He didn't say anything. And I didn't say anything, either. And now, wrapped in the silence that went on and on, I wondered if it wasn't really best to not look too deeply into things in silence, a little like swamp water that hadn't been stirred up, and which would be all the clearer because of the stillness, whereas in the last years you would've thought that all the mud had been churned up to the surface, along with the kinds of images that occur to me when I think of clear water. I often thought I would be perfectly happy being like the surface of a lake, but the judge didn't. He wanted me to go deeper, down to where things sleep or slither or crumple like tectonic plates. He wanted to drill down, to catch sight of essential oil, or something. He wanted to do that and I didn't. I told him several times that everything was right here under our eyes, and that it was a mistake to try and go back to some time that was dead, or defective, or defunct, in any case a time that wouldn't bring back the hours and the shames. What would there be to bring back? I asked.

A ghost, he said.

Yeah, a ghost, I guess.

I wanted to stand up then and fold my hands behind my back like an old sage explaining life to his disciple. Instead I stayed sitting across from him, just turning my head to look at the dozens of civil and maritime codes on the bookshelves, which seemed to contain all the answers on earth, their dark red and wine-colored covers gradually fading in our rare sunshine. Then he spoke more calmly, almost whispering this time, as if I were a wild animal he didn't want to frighten, and repeated his question: For heaven's sake, Kermeur, what were you thinking?

So I asked him: Do you know the story of the guy who almost won the lottery? It's pretty rare to know someone who won the lottery, right? But isn't it even rarer to know someone who almost won? Picture this: For ten years this guy plays the same numbers every week without fail, and then it happens, the day his six numbers came up is the one day he forgot to register his ticket. And it's true, it's unbelievable. There's one chance out of thirteen million of winning the lottery, and about the same odds of this guy forgetting to register his ticket, and the guy managed to multiply one by the other. I know someone this happened to, and it wasn't a neighbor or uncle: It was me.

Each week for years I kept a properly registered, carefully folded lottery ticket deep in my pocket, I told the judge. I would often touch it during the day, to make myself believe that some evening I would finally be a millionaire. And each week, Erwan, France, and I would sit down in front of the TV to watch the drawing broadcast, to watch the smiling girl on-screen announce the winning numbers, and then life would resume its normal course, that is, the course it never left, except that I left it every day, all week long, wanting to believe, each time I put my hand in my pocket, touching the ticket that for some reason, or for no reason, in any case, I knew for sure I hadn't registered.

So on Saturday the three of us are on the sofa as usual in front of the TV, as usual we aren't going to win the lottery, and we're happy. So I must've looked strange when the first number came up, then the second number, and the third, and I turned pale when I remembered that that morning, no, I can't believe it, that morning, this can't be real, it's impossible, but it was too late, and when the sixth number came up, it was much too late.

The look on Erwan's face, who didn't know. The look on France's face, who was on her feet saying, It's true, right there on the screen, those are our numbers. So without moving or looking at anyone I said, I didn't register the ticket.

The silence that followed. The girl on-screen smiling stupidly, repeating the numbers, 2, 5, 12, 24, 27, 31, and the bonus number, 7 of course, the bonus 7, and the girl on the screen, smiling as she looked at us.

After that, I don't know. France picked up the remote, pressed the button, and went out to the kitchen. She didn't say anything. Erwan and I wound up sitting together in front of the switched-off television. Erwan and I reflected in the gray screen, our faces hard to see because of the dust. I remember we stayed a moment like that, switched off, too.

It's no big deal, I tried to say, It's no big deal. I kept on trying to say it more and more quietly, more and more falsely, sinking deeper and deeper into the sofa, my body would've melted into the cushions if it could have, an apple in my throat going up and down with emotion, and the strange urge to check again to see if by any chance, if out of habit I actually had registered the ticket, because I didn't believe it right away. I went to bed without believing it. I tried to tell myself that it wouldn't change anything. I tried to tell myself that winning changes your life, but that losing, well, losing is what's usual, it wouldn't change anything because that's the usual. But there's losing, and then there's losing. And how can you tell if that or something else, if destiny can change for so little, not even knowing if you can say "so little" for a reversal of fortune so stinging it makes your head hurt for so long, because it's never the same, see, to have someone tell you the story as for it to happen to you on a sofa on a Saturday evening.

What about your wife? asked the judge.

My wife, nothing. My wife, not a word. Maybe there was already trouble brewing, I don't know, and I'm not saying this played a part in her leaving, I don't know if some sort of crack opened up that day, but the fact is, it's true that everything went to pieces around then, considering that if you look at life carefully everything converges at a few points and the rest of the time, nothing, or rather yes, the rest of the time you're left holding the bag.

In any case, today that's the way I see the last decade as I'm pulling all the lines together here in front of you, and it's like a kite whose strings I would tug on from a beach, as if suddenly I had a clear and almost supernatural view of the time passing, but it's always easy, looking back, to weave things into a destiny and then mark out the years with something like stakes or corner posts, and even a color to give them their final hue. Only when you're in it, in each year begun with a bottle of champagne, there's never a road map handed out on New Year's Day to lead us through the future. Never anything but the slightly fuzzy lines each of us tries to sketch to follow the course of the seasons, and that's all. The whole problem is that you have to take the curves yourself. Although where I'm concerned, I didn't feel I'd taken many curves. That's the advantage of stupidity: You just stand in the intersection waiting for a car to run you over. I mean, was I the one who decided from one day to the next that my wife should leave almost without warning? Was I the one who decided to lay off three-quarters of the workers at the Arsenal?

In any case, she found someone, I told the judge. France found someone, a new companion. That's the way she said it, "a new companion," standing at the door when she came to fetch Erwan for the weekend, and if by chance I invited her inside, in any case she would refuse.

So Erwan was living with you? asked the judge.

Yes, Erwan lived with me. It was his choice, to live with me. Don't ask me why. That's the way it is. I only know that France never liked it. Just imagine: a mother, her son. And he chooses his father. So maybe her "new companion" was her way of coming out on top. When she spoke about him, her new companion, I was never able to tell if it was out of embarrassment or pity for me, or maybe just pride: pride at having made the right decision, to not stay stuck with me, and today, with all the hours of loneliness when I felt she was beating me over the head with a spade, I can say she did well, more than well.

Your Honor, the only thing I don't want to know is whether it started before.

If what started before?

Her affair with him. Her new companion. Because after all she's the one who left, remember, so I have the right to wonder, you understand, I have the right to wonder how long, I'm sorry to say it like this, but how long she'd been going to his bedroom.

But that didn't seem to interest the judge, who was as indifferent as a doctor to his patients' complaints. I've since thought that doctors and judges are people who don't deal in feelings, quite the contrary, they're too busy pushing the branches aside and breaking through the understory they inhabit. Sometimes when the judge looked at me, you'd have thought he had a machete in his eyes and was using it to hack his way into me, as if he was aiming for some central point I didn't know myself, something that he might've simply called "the facts" and because he thought the truth was inside them, inside "the facts." As if truth would step out of the water all alone, dry and unwrinkled. And after all, why not?

When you come right down to it, I'll never know if there was a connection between the lottery ticket and France's leaving. I couldn't say there was, or rather I could say, but it bothers me too much. What I do know is that the four or five years that followed were certainly the stupidest of my life, if only you can call stupidity the hours of absence from one's self. The fact is that France left, and I never played the lottery again, because I know that kind of luck doesn't happen twice in a lifetime.

Unless some balding guy asks you out for a beer and talks about the future, said the judge.

Yes, except in that case. Except that this time the lottery ticket cost five hundred thousand francs.

And in a way, the drawing never happened, he said.

Yes, that's right, it never happened.

It'll be six years now, I said. Six years since I wrote a check for five hundred and twelve thousand francs to one Antoine Lazenec.

As I said those words, I would have wanted to gulp down a hundred gallons of air, the office suddenly felt even smaller, maybe because the afternoon was wearing on and the light was fading and the judge hadn't yet turned on the lamps that would soon light up our faces. There in the shadows, even what was being said began to darken, as if each minute had its own thickness, its rough density, and was an obstacle to time itself, as if being there talking and thinking and seeing so many images being carelessly mixed together, time itself was being accumulated and entangled in all the days gone by, as if I had gradually stopped recognizing anything of the fossilized days except the sticky, almost shapeless mass of the past.

You wrote a check, just like that? asked the judge. For five hundred and twelve thousand francs?

You must think I'm stupid, I answered. Of course not. Of course I didn't write a check just like that on the corner of a table in some restaurant. No, we did it all properly, before a *notaire* and all. Before a notaire, I repeated, as if I were unfolding the expression on the judge's desk like an old marine chart. That's right, before a notaire, in other words before a sworn officer of the court who could go to jail if he lets you sign something stupid. I remember, Lazenec and I were in the waiting room, with me pretending to read *Figaro Magazine* and Lazenec holding *Paris Match* when the notaire called us in. He stuck his head out the door, with his gray hair parted on the side like all the notaires in France, and said, "You're next," as if we were at the dentist's or the barber's. Sitting across from this man who wouldn't smile once in the next two hours, I had the feeling of being in front of the law in person. Do you understand? The law in person—that must mean something to you, I told the judge.

We sat on two plastic chairs facing the notaire's mahogany desk, and he read almost the entire grant deed, according to which I was indeed signing for a three-bedroom apartment with an ocean view, fourth floor, in Les Grands Sables apartment building, to be delivered within two years, with stipulations and clauses you can't imagine, paragraphs that protect you from everything: fire, flood, banks, hidden defects, and natural catastrophes.

And do you know what Lazenec said right there in the notaire's office, at the very moment when he was about to sign the deed with his Montblanc fountain pen? He said,

Contracts are like marriage, Kermeur, they're mainly useful in case of divorce.

I initialed forty-nine pages in triplicate that day. In other words, I carefully wrote M.K. for Martial Kermeur exactly one hundred and forty-seven times, and wrote my full signature at the end of each section, with very serious phrases like "Read and approved," "Certified on my honor," and "Signed and agreed."

When I left there two hours later with my signed and stamped grant deed, it felt like I'd had the Shroud of Turin authenticated by Christ in person. As I made my way home, with my fifty pages still warm with our three signatures, you mustn't think I regretted what I'd done, signing without really understanding. Quite the contrary. I walked into my house proudly, laid the contract on the table, and spent the entire evening reading it in detail. I remember Erwan was there, of course, so I quickly made dinner, and we sat down to eat as usual. And he could have talked to me about anything he wanted that evening, and I'm sure I wouldn't have heard a word of it.

I didn't tell Erwan anything. I didn't tell him anything for a long time. That's strange, now that I think of it. But then again, why would I go putting stories like that in the head of an eleven-year-old kid?

Is silence like darkness? I wonder about that now. Is it a too favorable climate for mushrooms and bad thoughts? Today, of course, I'd gladly say that plants and flowers blossom in the light of day, that you have to talk, see, you have to talk and shine light everywhere, in all children's lives, you can't let night or anxiety win. I now know how you transmit so many bad things to a son, I told the judge, if underneath the things you're saying there's so much charged air going from one of you to the other, in that porosity of things circulating in a kitchen at night when you're having dinner across from each other, and it may be in the fabric woven over the course of days, all those meals when he would tell me what he did in school and what kind of job he wanted later on, all those evenings when I wasn't really listening to him, it works like an underground water table seeking an outlet, believe me. And you're sitting there like an absentminded rock, there's no point in even trying to lie, no point in saying, "Yes, of course I'm listening to you," because like every child, he knows perfectly well when you're not listening, forever repeating some loop in his mind, like a sheet of glass in front of your eyes that cuts you off from the world, and then the more your thinking seems to wall you in, you may not realize it, but the more you're abandoning your child right then and there.

So you signed, said the judge. What then?

Then? Then nothing. Then zip, nothing at all, otherwise I wouldn't be here. Otherwise I'd be in a chaise longue with a blanket over my knees, gazing out at the ocean. I wouldn't be sitting across from you, trailing a string of pots and pans that jangle every time I make a move.

I heaved a deep sigh and moved my chair closer; it squeaked on the old parquet floor.

The thing I'll never know, I told the judge, the thing I'm dying to know, is just how much Lazenec knew. When did he realize that everything would come to a stop before so much as a concrete foundation was poured outside my window, that excavators would just do some digging, and after that, instead of stone blocks and windows being raised while we watched, instead of a six-story building with a terrace on the roof and an indoor pool, instead of all that there was a rectangular hole in the ground, an empty rectangle outlining a theoretical future, but only theoretical.

The judge flipped through his case files, pulled a bunch of photos from the folders, and laid them out in front of me.

They showed the progress of construction on the estate, if you could still call it an estate—what used to be an estate. Looking at them, the photographs were like evidence of the massacre, of building stones abandoned, the plowed-up five acres facing the sea, with just a few stakes and corner posts to mark out a construction site, and then a hole, a rectangle of emptiness like a new quarry being mined for valuable ore and nothing else, nothing, except for the soggy advertising posters hung on the chain-link fence still promising a bright future, with the irony far beyond them, the lawn turned to mud around the ruins of the château—ruins, of course, because when it came to destroying things, that was something Lazenec knew how to do.

Some of the photos showed a cement mixer or two badly framed against the sky, or people in the distance apparently having a conversation. Lazenec was in some of them, smiling away, as he did for so many years, the way he would smile and clap everyone on the back, and, like a Marseillais, hug and kiss people at random. On the job site he wore a suit and tie with a hard hat, but look, nobody needed a hard hat because there wasn't anything there.

Since then, instead of bags of mortar and rows of cinder blocks being laid, I told the judge, the only things that came together were the weeks and months and years, fitted into a compact and increasingly opaque block, only this one was horizontal. I watched this heavy time pass, being stacked up like a building erected under our very eyes, but it was the kind of building that wasn't likely to be demolished once it was up.

Time itself appeared like a ghost in the photographs, the city balconies in the distance an arena where spectators might have waited for the outcome of a battle between Lazenec and his own shadow. That shadow still hovered over the ruins, if you can call ruins the remains of something that hadn't happened. And my little house at the entrance to the estate, the five hundred square feet of stone I shared with Erwan, stood trembling in the middle of the disaster, surrounded by bulldozer scars, with red and ocher dust coming in the windows and getting into everything, our bedrooms, under our sheets, and on the toys gradually being moved up to the attic.

I didn't need to tell Erwan much, you understand. As time went on, he got it. As time went on, he could feel my worry growing, he saw my expression change over the months and seemed to sympathize when I looked out at the non-progress of the non-construction site, interrupted only by Lazenec's regular visits, tramping like a wild boar though a field of flowers, leading his useless guys and make-believe businesses around like walk-ons being paid to play the same scene every day. And of course he kept giving us big friendly waves when he saw Erwan or me at our kitchen window like plastic figurines with fixed smiles.

Do you know which fable Erwan learned at school that year? I asked the judge. It was "The Fox and the Crow." And when he recited it to me, each time he got to the sentence "It

ned its beak wide, and down fell the cheese," I swear that
omething cramped inside me. Like I was perched in a tree
and Lazenec was down below, looking at me and laughing
and saying, "This lesson's certainly worth a piece of cheese,
right?" So the more time went by, the less I felt like explaining things to Erwan. As time went on, it was as if I risked
accidentally dumping all the weight piled on my shoulders
onto his back. So by keeping quiet about my bad thoughts,
I was protecting him, as if I'd managed to build a water-
tight barrier between the two of us and the world, with me
sinking deeper and deeper in the mud of a stalled construction site, and him simply remaining a child. But it doesn't
work that way, does it? Maybe even childhood doesn't exist.
Maybe the world affects you at every age, and that's just the
way it is. Only when certain hours come, they're like black
marks that shape you.

Erwan in front of the switched-off television. Erwan in
the kitchen watching me think. Erwan outside the bank's
windows. Erwan behind his bedroom door. Erwan on the
docks looking at Lazenec's big boat. I'm saying that each
scene became a fixed image in his brain, like a box cutter
ripping his skin, or not his skin but slicing the flesh underneath, so it wound up lacerating his inner face. Maybe that's
all memory is, the sharp edges of inner images, not the images themselves, I mean, but the slashing jumble of images
inside us, chained up to keep them from getting loose, but
the chafing that stretches and holds them becomes like a

vulture tearing at your flesh, and without a devil or a god free you, the agony can last for years.

I was quiet for a moment. Erwan's face was floating there in the room between the judge and me. The judge himself seemed to be accompanying me in my thoughts.

I'd like to ask you something, I said.

Go ahead.

If you'd had to sentence Erwan, what would you do?

He nodded slowly and raised his left eyebrow, then said, I don't know, he really did screw up.

That's for sure, I said, it was a major screw-up.

And then a little more silence fell, maybe as a way to fill the distance between me and Erwan, a hologram suddenly pacing in his cell, there on the judge's desk between the books and the files, which had become like the walls of a prison.

The judge didn't move. As time went on, I started feeling I was in the office of a psychologist or someone like that, seeing him motionless, not answering, his hands folded under his chin, and because in the hours that had passed I felt he'd been asking me to dig inside myself the way a psychologist would have done, to unearth everything down to the dust of bones, provided it shed light, and even more light, and without wondering whether with too much light, people like me might go blind. God knows I knew that feeling of treating my brain like a stone quarry and excavating day after day to get out what I could, hoping it would eventually free me from searching too much, that I would eventually do something other than just watch the boats setting off at dawn and the outbound fishermen waving in a gesture of forgiveness—the fishermen being the guys from the Arsenal who'd been laid off, and the moment the money was in their bank accounts had run to the boat salesman and without hesitating, without arguing, pointed at the one they'd been coveting for years, because they knew how to do that, like a gift or a genetic program inscribed in them, they'd been able to do it, nursing that fixed, patient thought, and when the time was right, circulating it in their nerves and not just in their nerves but right down to their index finger pointing at this or that model, saying: That one, I want that one. But for me, it was as if I lacked that program.

And now that the château had been razed, now that I could see the sea directly from my kitchen window, each time one or another of them hailed us from his cockpit, their lobster traps ready to be set, I had the impression they were taunting Erwan and me as we stood behind the window and looked at the sea. Sometimes Erwan asked me: Why don't you buy yourself a boat? Looking totally evasive, I would tell him: Sure, of course I'm going to buy one, I'm going to buy one very soon. And to help convince him, I took him to the port to look at boats that very afternoon, and we visited sales offices, comparing prices. He was twelve, maybe fourteen, his voice starting to change. After so many worn-out promises, I could almost hear him saying: I know you'll never buy anything, I know you've never been able to make a decision, but don't forget that someday someone will make a decision for you, and when that time comes, they won't ask your opinion about it.

I read this in Erwan's nonchalance, now that he had reversed our roles, I mean in the beginning I was the one who took him along, and then little by little he forced himself to go with me, as if to make me happy, or even worse, so as not to broadcast his pity or his shame everywhere, because I now know that whatever take you might have on a problem, a son doesn't want to see that, your weakness. A son isn't programmed to pity you.

In a way, it would've been easier if Lazenec had just skipped out, left the area and changed his name. We would've run from law firm to law firm filing hopeless suits against the bankers, the insurers, and the notaires connected with the project, at least it would've kept us busy. We would've lost, but we would've been busy. I'll say it again: Lazenec's stroke of genius was to go on living among us, staying all those years, summer and winter, like he was a flower, a sunflower that turns as the hours pass, in a garden contest where he took first prize. And do you know why? Because the longer he stayed, the more we told ourselves that if he's staying, for sure it means that he's not dishonest. If he stays, it means he believes in the project. Whereas it was actually just the opposite: He stayed so the rest of us would keep on believing, so he could fan our little inner fire every day, walk around each person's soul, stoking their boiler with overflowing shovelfuls of some inexhaustible fuel. And it worked. Because the funniest thing isn't even that a guy was able to hypnotize an entire village, the funniest thing is how much time it took us to come back from that strange country, to have written a check that big, to watch the guy who cashed it spending money like there was no tomorrow, and still tell ourselves that this was a sign that we'd put our money in good hands. And do you know why? Because it meant that he had money, it meant that things were working, and it meant that soon, very soon, it would be our turn to play with fat rolls of bills. Think of what that means, for a guy like me to be saying this, as though I were the kind of person who wanted to play with rolls of bills. Not that I suddenly started liking those nouveau riche manners, but I just got used to them, I wound up thinking it was normal that Lazenec should spend his days in the best restaurants, without telling myself that it was our money in his hands and in his pockets, our money that he was cheerfully burning through or shifting from one account to another like the coins in a shell game.

This all might seem crazy to you, and that's understandable because you look at facts, just the facts, but you can line them up one after another on a timeline, and it still doesn't explain this. To understand, to really understand deep down, we need a new science or new physics, with a new Einstein who would explain how the soul or thought or, I don't know, this thing inside that vibrates in the light, this thing that sings its own music, with notes that the ear can't hear, those deep strange notes like the song of humpback whales. That's it, Lazenec and I were humpback whales and our waves met under the ocean.

And it's not as if I hadn't taken him aside a thousand times to ask when the project would really get going, and even, more than once, to suggest that it would be better if we just backed off and settled it as friends: We'll tear up the contract, I'd say, you give me back my money and that'll be the end of it. But you know what he answered, besides the hundred times when he brushed me off with a pat on the shoulder? He said, "I'm concerned, Kermeur. You aren't broke, are you?"

That's completely nuts, wouldn't you say? The very guy who caused you to be broke is now handing you a pole longer than his arm, he's opening the door so you can shout whatever you want right into his ear, and instead of that, you quietly answer, "No, of course not, I'm not broke, but still, you understand..." Whereas of course you're broke. You saw your banker just the day before about a huge overdraft, you watched your son waiting outside the bank windows kicking an empty can while you were promising the banker that things would be all right, that you had faith in the project and the guy behind it, so that the whole scene of you begging the banker, of you feeling your breath coming a little shorter each day, is playing out while Lazenec's question is hanging in the air, but instead of that, you again say, No, of course not. And you just add that after all this time you're starting to get a little worried. But a guy like him takes the phrase "a little" and gauges how much room he still has to maneuver, measures it with his own instruments, and those instruments have strange names. I'm pretty sure they're called "instinct," and "intuition," and "cunning."

For a little guy like me to be taken to the cleaners, that's just the way things are, I told the judge, but for the others, the people in the city or the soccer club, people who invested ten times as much as I did, it's completely crazy.

How many units, did you say?

Thirty. Thirty units. Thirty apartments at an average of five hundred thousand francs each is a pretty good chunk of change, isn't it?

At that point something in the judge seemed to gradually stiffen, as if I had an electric transformer and was slowly turning up the power. Now more and more angry, he exclaimed: For God's sake, what could he have done with all that money?

What do you think he did with it? I asked. He spent it! He spent it, with the rest of us watching him. Right under the noses of thirty suckers like me who dropped five hundred thousand francs on a scale model. He burned through that money right under my nose, under the mayor's nose, under Erwan's nose. It's not hard to figure out, he burned through that money right in front of us. I've drunk some great wines too, but you know what money I used? The money for a Merry Fisher that I never bought, whereas he did. That's right, Lazenec bought a brand-new Merry Fisher and even went so far as to take us out for cruises around the harbor.

The judge tried to calm down, several times picking up the pen he'd been playing with for hours, to make a note of something or just to look busy.

So there were thirty of you, he said. What about the twenty-nine others?

Oh yeah, the other twenty-nine, that's right. Well, the twenty-nine others should be here with me facing you. I mean they should have helped me toss Lazenec into the drink. Because I don't mind telling you, it's not so easy to heave somebody over a boat railing all by yourself.

The judge didn't pick up on that, didn't ask exactly how I'd done it, how I waited for us to stop the boat, for us to haul up the pot with the lobster and the crabs, how Lazenec leaned over to lower it to the bottom again, sixty feet down. Standing behind him, all I had to do was to grab him by the legs and dump him into the sea like a sack of potatoes. That was all there was to it, that's how it happened.

But the judge wasn't interested in those details. What interested him was something more mental, like a math equation he had to formulate or solve. But I needed to solve the puzzle too, I told him, only I'm not a thinker, so I need to solve it physically. And I'm not an impulsive person, either, if you figure what six years of daily patience represents, six years of believing that instead of getting a bad mushroom, there might be an apartment with bay windows glinting in the sun.

Okay, said the judge, but about the twenty-nine others: Why didn't you get together against Lazenec?

Because, I said. And like an eight-year-old, I ended the sentence as soon it was out, just repeating a little more quietly, "Because."

Because what?

Because I didn't want people to know.

In the silence of the photos spread in front of us, my shame seemed to swell up like an inner tube, my shame at never telling anyone anything, because I, the 1981 Socialist, had invested all my cash in a real estate project. That's something you can't understand, I told the judge, but I just couldn't talk about it, I couldn't admit that I'd put my entire layoff bonus into a real estate venture. Not an old Socialist like me, do you understand?

But I gather there were some other guys like you who also lost their bonuses, he said.

Yeah, but guys like me, as you say, they weren't any more visible than I was. Each of us was hunkered down in the silence of his own trap. Best not to know the list of people who were taken in—guys like me, sure, who were no quicker than me to notice a gloved hand gently reaching into their wallet. I'm not saying it was a good thing that we kept quiet. I'm only saying that it was us. So for a long time, nobody knew. Not Erwan. Not France. Not Le Goff. For a long time, each of us lived all alone with a well yawning under our feet and just a flimsy grille covering it. What I'm saying is that getting rid of a guy like that was acting for the common good.

His elbows propped on the desk, the judge silently looked at each photo of the disaster and spread them out in front of him—the mud, the sea, the sky—like they were postcards he might've brought back from various trips, or a losing hand he'd laid down in some poker game.

Look there, I said, that's him with my son, Erwan.

They look like they're getting along, said the judge.

You take a twelve-year-old kid and a guy with a Porsche who drives him to stadium suites to watch his favorite soccer team, what do you think's going to happen?

It probably went on for two years, Lazenec's habit of swinging by our place to pick up Erwan and take him along. Maybe you think he did it to make amends, because my money had long ago gone up in smoke, right? No, it wasn't even that. Because the problem is that even with a bad guy, even the worst of bastards, there are times when he's not a bastard, times when he's not looking to do harm. And believe me, that doesn't make things easy for people like me. People like me need logic, and logic says that a bad guy should be bad all the time, not just a third of the time. In fact, maybe it's even worse than that. Maybe the guy never thought of doing anything evil, really evil, the evil that's written deep down in each of us. Maybe there's always something that justifies and absolves it, or erases it. I mean this guy followed his line, and the line told him to sell apartments, to sit on café terraces and pitch them, and his line told him that taking other people's money would cause him no pain. So maybe that's the same line that led him to become fond of Erwan, to the point of picking him up for soccer games, except that he honked from the end of the path because he didn't want to face me too often. Not that he was the kind to slink around, in spite of all the times I pestered him to find out if things were moving and if we could hope that soon, yes soon, maybe after two years or three years…I still believed in it as much as I did the very first day, I had total faith. Something in me would say: Of course for a project like this, three years is nothing surprising, what with all the codes to meet and the signatures to get, of course it's normal. And Lazenec knew how to feed the flame. If you ever got more curious, if for some reason you started asking about techniques or materials, he would talk about this crooked supplier or that building code keeping him from moving ahead, and it was like a game of blindman's buff that he won every time. All that worked on me, Your Honor, patience and obstacles swept away with each smiling promise, so just imagine the effect it had on a twelve-year-old kid.

I fell silent again for a moment, to give the judge time to picture it. Then I asked, Do you have children too?

He said: Yes, I have a son.

I wish you all the best for him.

The judge nodded a few times, his head moving up and down like an automaton I'd wound up with the key in his back. His face took on a kind of brotherly expression, and instead of him being a judge and me a guy under arrest, we were just two fathers facing each other and projecting our stories into each other's eyes.

One thing's for sure, though: That boy, that little Erwan who looked up at me to see if it was okay to get into Monsieur Lazenec's Porsche, he doesn't exist anymore. Today he would be more likely to smash the Porsche into a wall if he saw it on the village streets with the window wide open and the same old Lazenec waving broadly to everyone right and left. Because if one person hasn't changed up until today, it's Lazenec.

Until yesterday, the judge corrected me.

I'm sorry, that's right, until yesterday. Up until yesterday he was like a king on the church square, and he continued to swagger in front of us, his creditors, and even then, even after five or six years and his reputation getting around like a yellow snake at the bottom of the harbor, he would still manage to find yet another innocent sparrow to write him a nice little check. And the money continued to leap from one saddle to the other because there was always a new horse joining the race to make the last link of the chain. But you know the rule, I said to the judge: A chain is only as strong as its weakest link. And if one of them breaks, it doesn't hold, and your boat drifts away in the night. With a little luck, you wake up at dawn out at sea, in the slanting sunrise. But it's just as likely that in the hour after the break you hear the terrible crash of the hull being driven onto the rocks, water pouring into the cabin, and at best, at the very best, you're able to swim to shore.

Don't blame me, but sometimes I have strange images that come to mind, I told the judge. They never last for long; it passes. But as long as they're there, I stare vacantly, my eyes turned to a screen that had come down inside me, and you have to wait. So the judge waited. And in my head, it was like an iron frame with right angles tearing at time.

The judge never seemed bothered by those long empty seconds that punctuated what I said, when in my head certain sentences left a fixed plan in their wake, an image that lasted and couldn't be erased anymore.

I don't blame you for not understanding, I said, given how long it took me to understand, to put the right words to this whole mechanism, but now I get it, I understand how he managed to stay among us in his Porsche and all the restaurants of the city. Basically, the more absurdly you act, the more room for maneuvering you have because as long as the person opposite you hasn't keyed that into his calculator, as long as he hasn't built a little machine to tame the absurdity, he's paralyzed. Great boxers know this, that it's only when their opponent's game is in their box, that is, only when it's finally locked in their brain like on a little music-box turntable, only then do they know how to fight, but before that you just take punches, and that's all. And the more punches you take, the less lucid you are, and the less lucid you are, the more punches you take, you understand? Go to Le Goff's grave and ask him what he thinks of this.

The judge leaned back in his leather armchair, sighed wearily, and asked: But hadn't Le Goff invested too?

Le Goff is a bit more complicated, Your Honor.

And I fell silent again, with Le Goff hanging like a projected slide in the wave of air circulating between heaven and my chair, and it refused to leave the screen too quickly.

I think it's Catherine's face that first comes up for me when I say Le Goff's name. Especially the tears streaming down her cheeks on the day of the funeral. She did everything she could, I told the judge, everything a wife could do to keep her husband from falling down the well. Except that a moment comes when there's nothing you can do for somebody, no way to pull them out, even though they're shouting, "Save me!" Because their whole body is pulling them in the other direction, and there's nothing you can do against the broken glass we drag behind us, a bit like the sound of a mirror rattling on the wall, a sound that's sometimes impossible to fight. I think that with Le Goff, that noise had long been getting louder and louder, all those times he came to my place to see for himself how the work was going, coming more and more often, as if we were two soldiers taking turns on guard duty at my kitchen window, two soldiers looking through binoculars to see if the enemy was on the move. And for a long time, Le Goff put a good face on it. For a long time, our optimism continued to float above the rubble and the bulldozer tracks, even those many times when we sat smoking on my terrace, watching as excavators knocked the trees down one after another. We felt upset, seeing the machines do their work, but we both kept looking to the future.

I never told Le Goff I'd invested, never mentioned the fourth-floor three-bedroom place with an ocean view. Of course not. To the contrary, I would tell him, This whole project is good for the commune, but it really doesn't concern me. As I tried to face him with my own lie, I watched new worry lines appear on his forehead as the months passed. Seeing him on my terrace, smiling, or in the newspapers with Antoine Lazenec, reassured me, of course. After all, he had endorsed the sale of the property. After all, he was the mayor.

Martial thought he was doing the right thing. And so did we, most of us, that is, from the town council to the café tables, everybody followed his lead because he thought he was acting like a man of his times, and what were his times? A shipyard closing and the promise of a future, so he insisted that for the rest of us, us leftists, it was time to change.

And for changing, we sure changed. Him even faster than me, becoming more and more somber, preoccupied, and oppressed. You could measure it by the growing redness of his cheeks as he began spending more and more time in bars. For a mayor, it's true that he was always happy to toss one down, but over time we could tell this was different, with Catherine herself going to fetch him from the back of some café. After those last two years, do you know what he looked like? Maybe an old sea captain who starts to realize that he isn't in command of anything anymore, that even the movement of the tides has stopped in his mind, leaving seaweed to spread in his brain. That's the way Le Goff seems to me now, like his head was polluted with dirty, stagnant water.

I'd wished he'd stop coming by, stop standing in my garden telling me a thousand things I'd rather not know, except it was clear that the rattle of the mirror in his skull was gradually rising to a roar like a waterfall crashing on rocks, and that in the course of time I began to understand, yes, understand—this will sound stupid—the opacity of things.

And then of course there was one time too many.

There's always a last time, isn't there? And of course we call it the one time too many because it's the last one. But the fact is, he came over one November evening, I saw him approaching like a shadow staggering along the path, muttering stuff I couldn't make out. Just from the way he was walking, I could tell that it wasn't as usual. It was one time too many, his standing out against the white gravel. His wandering the peninsula one time too many.

It didn't take me long to realize that it wasn't the wind that was making Le Goff walk like that but lord knows how many glasses he'd drunk alone in his office. I began to understand the words he was saying in his hoarse voice: that he was the lowest of the low, that he'd really been screwed, that we'd all been screwed. And then he saw me in the distance and seemed to stagger a little less, as if he had a direction to take and it straightened him up, as if I were a beacon in his darkness. He picked up his pace toward me, and when he was still a few yards away in the darkness, he started shouting, You've been screwed too, Kermeur, you've been screwed big-time.

Hearing him that way, it felt as if the trees in the dusk looked darker and more tangled than usual and seemed to be falling on me, as if there were a persistent, mocking rumor snaking through the air. I had the impression that the pines and the ferns and the thick dune grass, all of them proud to be living in their world, a world without an evil word or thought, had a secret they were whispering about me. I would've liked to have been a tree that day, you know. And Le Goff was still coming closer, still shouting those awful things into the falling night, saying, "Kermeur, you were no better than the rest," and after all these years, it was the first time he used the familiar "*tu*" with me.

I heard a shutter squeak shut not far off, and a couple of lights seemed to go out at the same time, and I thought I would've liked to close my own shutters right then, see- ing as how Le Goff kept shouting my name in the damp air, and that I was never more conscious that my name was Kermeur. He seemed to be forcing himself to laugh between sentences and, as he got closer, this time more quietly, in a way more sarcastically, he stood in front of me and said, So you went and invested in real estate, eh?...You're the sly one...But you can't hide anything from the mayor, nope, nothing at all, the mayor sees everything, the mayor knows everything...

What's with you? I said. What are you talking about? You're completely drunk.

Le Goff went on: We all have our little secrets don't we?, while shifting from one leg to the other like a roly-poly toy, that's what he looked like that evening, a roly-poly who couldn't steady himself, trying to light a cigarette out of the wind under my porch roof and taking a drag as if it were pure oxygen. He pressed his face against my window to look inside to be sure I was alone, which I was. Erwan had gone to watch the game at the stadium and I'd quit going with him some time ago. Le Goff tried to crush out his cigarette, but the wind blew it away before his foot reached it.

There I was, standing with Le Goff, who was shouting all this nonsense to the rooftops, so what could I do? I invited him in. Don't stand there, I said, come inside. Which he did, he came into my house, and without being asked sat down, or I should say collapsed, on the sofa. I went to the kitchen to see what I could find to give him to drink and perhaps for me as well because I figured we were going to spend quite some time together and it might be best if we were in the same state. So I brought out a bottle of whiskey, that's right, whiskey, I told the judge. That evening I felt like having whiskey.

It sort of calmed him a little to sink into the sofa, his weight crushing the cushions, and I could see he was trying to get a grip and straighten up a little. He even started using the formal "*vous*" again. He said he was sorry that it was only like this, in this condition, that he could even come here, but that there weren't a lot of people he could talk to right now, and that I was the first person he had to apologize to.

Me? I asked.

I owe an apology to the whole town, he said, the whole town.

He didn't need to say much more for us to see the twisted shape of events appear right before our eyes, under the ceiling light, meaning the somewhat blurry collection of missing buildings, false smiles, and thousands of banknotes.

And I happen to know, he continued, your five hundred thousand francs, I know exactly where they are.

Well, so what? I asked. What difference does that make?

Oh, not much, he answered, not much. He poured himself another drink, stared into the bottom of his glass, and added, It's more like I'm here to help you kiss them goodbye.

Your Honor, I don't think I understood everything he meant by the phrase "kiss them goodbye," but in my head it felt like a huge tarp was being dragged over the whole peninsula, like a black tide rising from the bottom of the ocean to wash its filth all over the harbor. And it suited the wind that was blowing then, a wind that suddenly felt like a thickish, dark layer, and suited this impossible night where everything seemed to be hardening and orbiting some dark moon.

But the strangest thing was that Le Goff wasn't telling me anything new, more like he'd brought the last piece you put on top of a house of cards, the one you know will make everything collapse, but you long ago understood that each of the preceding stages led to this one, the collapse, so all I said, maybe out of pride too, all I said was, You're the mayor, Martial, it's up to you to do something.

Le Goff's eyes seemed to be having trouble focusing anywhere. He looked at me with pity, or the feeling that he was way ahead of me, and came out with this rather dry statement: Do something? No, there's nothing to do, it's been a long time since he staked me out like a tethered goat.

I didn't understand what he meant by that right away. What does "like a tethered goat" mean, Your Honor? But I have had time to understand since, and especially that a certain Antoine Lazenec already knew what it meant, and what a stake was, and that any town councillor in France could be turned into a goat or an ass and tied to it with a bridle around his neck. That he knew, all right. And for Le Goff, Lazenec didn't have to work hard to slip it over his head. It wasn't something to be splashed across the newspapers, more like a belt of explosives cinched good and tight around Le Goff's waist, and he better not try to loosen it or else it would blow up.

I don't quite understand, said the judge.

Well, let me talk. Let me finish and we'll see if you get it. Me, you better believe I understood pretty quickly, with the whiskey in my belly, my thinking took a shortcut that day, because in a flash that lit up my mind, I asked, So you invested too, Martial?

Le Goff raised his eyes to me, looking a little more directly, a little more heavily, and he stayed like that for a long time in silence.

The problem wasn't just that Le Goff had invested, Your Honor. He could've bought ten apartments if he'd felt like it. The problem was that he'd invested all right—but not his own money.

No. The town's money. He invested the town's money, you see? He put down payments on ten apartments pretty much like me, except that ten times five hundred thousand francs comes to five million, and for a commune like ours, five million francs is the chasm between solvency and bankruptcy. That was the thing Le Goff had come to tell me that evening, that he had bankrupted the town. I think that's how he put it: I bankrupted the town.

The word "heaven" came to my mind then, like a parasite that can't be eradicated, because of all the years that had seen it wilt and rot where it stood. I could now see the word "heaven" in the living room, cracked all over, banging against the windows, falling apart and fading, as if it was soon going to slide under the closed door and spread its stench over the whole harbor. In the silence weighing on us, Le Goff made a sound with his mouth, a kind of "pff!" and opened his outstretched hand to say that the money, all the money, had evaporated, pff! And then, suddenly sober, he looked at me as if he was going to make a serious announcement during a town council session, and concluded: I fucked everything up.

So just imagine: Me, who'd never been more than a poor guy caught up in the same story as him, suddenly he was confiding everything to me, as if we were brothers or, I don't know, that through the liquor and the resignation amplifying each other, Le Goff no longer wanted to hide anything and it was as if all of his inner darkness was lit up by…I don't know, by…

Lucidity? said the judge.

Yes, that's exactly right, I said, lucidity. You always come up with the right word.

And now you're in the same boat as me, Le Goff said, and I'm sorry to say that this boat of ours, after twenty-five years of quietly cruising along the coast, has been taking on more water than it can handle. It might even be time to get off it.

I don't know what else Le Goff would've added, what tornado of words he would've pulled us into, if at that moment the door hadn't been yanked open, the wind suddenly blowing into the living room, and we saw Erwan standing in front of us, his fan scarf still tied around his neck.

We were startled, of course. I was surprised to see him, as if he had no business being there, as if he were still a kid asleep in his bedroom, whereas of course Erwan hadn't been a kid for a long time. I was able to forget the years that had just passed while Erwan went from eleven to seventeen without my seeing anything other than the pit yawning at my feet, and I had kind of forgotten him, forgotten that he was old enough to stay up late and go out alone and come home when he felt like it. But if one of us should have been surprised, it was him, to see us up at such an hour with the nearly empty whiskey bottle and the smell of our talk from the bottom of our glasses still hanging in the air.

If you'd seen the look he gave us at that moment, like we were two animals in a zoo, and him just saying, What is this shit? in his adult voice, I felt this was no time to argue. Erwan has grown up to be the nervous kind. You wouldn't have taken the handcuffs off him, Your Honor. He would've jumped at your throat to strangle you in a second. Fathers and sons aren't always alike, and if I've understood anything in this story, it's that at some point your children aren't an extension of yourself. But how many years it takes to realize that—not us so much, but them—how many years it takes them to eventually understand that they aren't the avenging sword of our dreams and all the things we haven't accomplished in life, that they're not here to clean up our messes?

The judge seemed to empathize, or at least his expression gave every sign of it.

How old is your son? I asked.

He's seven.

So you haven't gone through any of this yet.

He shook his head. No, not yet.

Seven years old, I went on. You know what happened to us when Erwan was seven? I'm pretty sure the whole city remembers. I'm not saying it explains anything but on that day, I nearly died in front of my own son, that's right, in front of Erwan and in front of the whole town, actually. I remember it like it was yesterday. A big Ferris wheel had been set up on the city hall square. I think it was the first year it was there, turning like that above us, its ring of cars like a big clock in the sky, so of course I suggested to Erwan that we take a spin. I bought two tickets, and we sat down facing each other, Erwan and me, on the round bench covered in fake red leather, and I told him not to move because it could be dangerous and because I've always had vertigo, even more for other people than for myself—especially with my own son—and the cars swinging in the wind and the city shrinking into an illustrated poster as we went up. You really got a great view of the city and our peninsula off in the distance and even our house probably in the middle of it, and this was before any question of divorce or Lazenec or all of that, and for a few minutes it was wonderful to be way up in the sky, with the ocean almost at our feet, yes it was wonderful. And then the car started back down. So when we got to the bottom near the wooden ramp, I naturally got out first to help Erwan down, and once on the ground I reached out to catch him. Only at that moment, when I almost had him in my arms, I don't know what the guy at the controls was thinking, he must've been looking somewhere else or something, but the Ferris wheel suddenly started moving again, and Erwan was thrown back into the car and I don't know what came over me, but seeing Erwan all alone above me, seeing him leaving without me, instead of letting him go, I reflexively grabbed the metal bar with both hands and started climbing too, only I was outside the car, just imagine, clinging to the iron bar by my arms and my whole body hanging in space, slowly rising like a hot-air balloon. When you look at it, a Ferris wheel goes up damn fast, I can tell you. Nobody realized what was happening except me, except me and of course Erwan, who started to scream and cry and pretty soon I was yelling like a wild man, Stop the machine, get me down, not to mention the string of curses I let loose. Loud music was blaring in the enclosures, and it drowned me and Erwan out, and the wind and the cold were increasing with every foot. I didn't know how many more seconds I could hang on like that while the wheel kept climbing and climbing like a kind of music-box cylinder playing its notes. I could see the people down below starting to look and wonder when I was going to fall. Pretty soon I was more than a quarter of the way up, maybe seventy or eighty feet in the air, so if I let go, I was a dead man for sure. Those moments where you're close to death don't happen very often, do they? I can promise you, a sort of infinity opens between survival and death, the kind of gulf you fill with all the anxiety you need to keep yourself in suspense while inventing any tricks your brain can come up with to even conceive of the idea of death. Today, I don't remember if I had time to think about all that then or if it was much later, but it remained like a breach that's yet to be filled, and I often tell myself that dying isn't so bad, that it would be over fast, I barely needed to believe that I would go on being part of the physical world, that I would become rock or sand or maybe part of me would still be here in a thousand years, turned into a plant, who knows? But I can tell you that I long ago ditched the idea that some part of me is going to rise into the air.

As for rising into the air, at that moment I was like a spring stretched toward the sky that was going to snap soon. All I knew was the infinite distance that would never be filled was written in Erwan's eyes, and his little child's hands were trying to circle my wrists, with me saying, No, Erwan, don't hold on to me, you'll fall too, let me go. But at seven, what could he know about his preference and his desire to go on living after me? In a sense, it was too late to explain all that to him, to reassure him that of course he could live without me, that any child can survive and grow up without a father, and looking back now, maybe that might have been for the best.

But here I am, in front of you. I didn't die that day because as I screamed, the guy in the car below us screamed in turn to the one lower down and it went from one to another until a big human chain of screams reached the ears of the guy at the controls to tell him what was happening and to stop everything and quickly send the wheel turning backward. So I felt the car stop and then very slowly start coming back down, the same movie running backward, as if we were going back in time, erasing it, that nothing had happened, I hadn't grabbed the iron bar, Erwan hadn't cried, we'd never gotten onto the Ferris wheel. I remember that feeling, and I'd like it if it were still possible to feel that sometime in our lives we could go backward.

Except you'll agree that in normal time, there's no reverse gear. I haven't seen anything that looked like that in my story, in any case, except to say that everything since then has been going counterclockwise, as if I'd fallen asleep that day at the very top of the Ferris wheel and haven't woken up, that since then I hear murmuring deep in my dreams, and Erwan hadn't yet grown up, I mean he hadn't yet seen his father slumped on the sofa year after year with a calculator instead of a brain, hitting the bottle with old friends who got redder and redder, and fatter and fatter. But Erwan has grown up since then. Erwan drinks whiskey and smokes cigarettes, and his shoulders are broader than mine.

He may well say I'm the one who has aged, that my neck is bowed with weariness at the sound of the thousand battles that should be fought, but in fact he's just starting to understand he's the one who has grown, that he no longer has to stand on tiptoe to kiss me, and he's discovering within himself the only thing that has to worry him: I'm his father, just me. That's something you learn when you're eighteen or twenty. That you will have the same father your whole life. That you will spend your life with the same ghosts. The same singers on the radio. The same politicians. And be stuck with the same childhood.

Erwan didn't stay with us for long. He spun on his heel and went to lock himself in his bedroom, turning up the music loud so we could hear. Le Goff and I almost burst out laughing, like two naughty boys caught in the act, each one held up by the other's giggling. But we heard the bedroom door slam and looked at each other, and we didn't laugh. Then Le Goff got up, awkwardly leaning on the soft sofa armrests, and said, a little wearily: I think I'm going to go now.

But what was strange was that now I didn't want him to leave. I don't know if it was the wind outside calling, or the feeling that my house was too small for our anger, or only that it wasn't all that late, but I wound up saying, I'll go with you, Martial, it'll do me good. And that's what we did. We stood up, kind of quickly. We put on our jackets and went out.

As we walked in the night wind, it became obvious that I'd caught up with Le Goff, that is to say that in the damp air I was as drunk as he was, and also as light as he was, with the liquor and the wind like two bookends holding us perfectly upright in the clear night.

There are two things I sometimes want to thank, I told the judge, and that's wind and liquor. That's right, liquor. It may shock you to hear me saying that, especially since you wouldn't have me drinking even a beer right now, but I'm telling you, liquor and wind make an exceptional combination. Never forget that on some evenings even the worst rotgut whiskey, the stuff that'll twist your guts all the next day, will fix your heart, it'll tear at your heart but it will fix it, drain it of all its toxins accumulated over the months that suddenly no longer circulate in your veins because they've been eliminated by gallons of liquor and lost sleep. You owe it to all those things you would only do at certain hours and when you're in a certain condition, all those thoughts you would only have at certain hours and in a certain condition, and those thoughts are like the most powerful detergent I know.

That same detergent led us down to the beach to look at the choppy sea. With all the wind outside and all the liquor inside us that night, it did us good to look at the sea and swear at Lazenec. We said we weren't going to give in to that asshole. We shouted at the ocean. That son of a bitch. And it was almost like a contest. That motherfucker. Each insult went skipping out over the water. That bastard. And the wind carried them far away. That fat prick.

When I got home later, I remember that Erwan was sitting there in the living room his legs crossed like in a waiting room, with that look of his as he waited for me, just as it was like me to very quietly turn my key in the lock so as not to wake him up, in case he'd been able to go to sleep. He was looking at the whiskey bottle like it was evidence against me. He asked what Le Goff had been doing there. What the fuck was he doing here? is what he said, exactly.

I don't know if it was meeting his gaze from that armchair, with his head now higher than its back, but hearing him talk to me like a father to his son caused something in me to crack. That's right, you heard me, a father to his son, because in opening the door, in stepping into my own house, I was suddenly a teenager who deserved a good hiding. It's as if I were the one tucked deep in his pocket now, because for sure that's where I would've wanted to be, hidden in the seam near his armpit, if only to escape the shame, or, I don't know, whatever feeling of unworthiness a father might have in front of his son.

Erwan poured himself a whiskey, and it felt weird to see my own son raising a glass of liquor to his lips.

None of this concerns you, I told him, this is grown-up stuff. If you were a normal boy you wouldn't be here waiting for me late on a Saturday night, you should be out with a girl, or I don't know, in a bar drinking beer with your pals, but not worrying about things that won't change your life. That's it, I said, at your age, you should focus on life-changing things.

He just went on drinking his whiskey and when he blew out a puff of cigarette smoke, his whole answer to me was written in the cloud in front of his face, without my being able to tell how much avoidance or insolence was in it. At that point, when we probably hadn't yet finished our conversation, we heard a shot in the night, a deep, heavy sound. I think I understood right away. I think I said: Le Goff.

It always happens, there comes a day and a time when things reach a tipping point and afterward you can't act as if it hadn't happened. It might just be one more grain of sand falling in the hourglass, but it's one grain too many, and after that nothing's the same, everything collapses or is renewed, with events falling one after another like the lines of a poem.

I think the shot could still be heard beneath the black umbrellas open over the tomb the following Friday, the bullet bouncing off the walls of the bell tower for at least three days and ricocheting in the tolling of the bell before whizzing down the cemetery paths. There, with the village gathered by the hundreds, its echo joined the beating of our hearts, the crunching of the gravel, and the pounding of the rain, because it was raining that day.

Lazenec was there, of course. I looked at him, with just the space of the open grave between us and the coffin slowly being lowered by the cemetery workers to its final resting place.

One thing's for sure, Your Honor, if you looked to see where the bullet that Le Goff put in his skull a few days earlier really came from, if you wanted to find the bullet's provenance in the facts, I mean the real provenance in thought, in the inner circuit of images and shames, it wouldn't take long to figure out who pulled the trigger.

I tossed a rose onto the coffin and so did the others, there were dozens of them and they fell like colored tears onto the black wood. A hard rain was falling, and each person paused for a moment in the rain: friends, neighboring mayors, townspeople, and of course Catherine, holding her hat with one hand because of the wind that was still blowing hard that day. France was there, too. Dressed in black, too. I don't dare say that France had class, because people like us definitely fall into that category called "ordinary people," but on that day, because of the black veil that covered her face, her high heels, and her velvet coat closed at the throat, I found her beautiful, without knowing what sparked that thought in me, or not really a thought, maybe a feeling, though I've never quite been able to distinguish between a thought and a feeling.

Afterward, France decided to not follow us to the mayoralty, where we'd organized a final tribute in the banquet hall. As was usual with her, France slipped away, and when Erwan and I looked around for her in the crowd coming from the cemetery, she had disappeared. On that day, even Erwan wasn't acting the rebellious adolescent who looked down on me, because I think Le Goff's death had shaken him, too. We walked side by side to the mayoralty, ignoring the rain, ignoring the dripping water soaking our shoes and our coats.

So there we were, back in the same hall that had once been so festive, and of course we helped get things ready and fill the empty glasses that were sitting on the paper napkins. I went to the storeroom to get a couple of bottles, and there in the corner stood the old Grands Sables model, all by itself. You could still see the tiny plastic people, who seemed to not have enough air to breathe, the dust gathering on the glass like condensation that would eventually asphyxiate them.

I brought the bottles out to the buffet table and we all ate our piece of brioche and drank our glass of cider, in one of those moments when we take a pause before resuming normal life, something to get us clear of death or the idea of death. At funerals we always dive into the grave with our dead and then invent a thousand strategies to back out and get shed of death, which seems to cling to our clothes for a long time. Antoine Lazenec was there, holding a glass of cider. I guarantee he was the only person to not have left anything in the grave, at least to judge by the way he was stuffing his face with brioche and curbing his smiles somewhat, out of respect. Our eyes met. In those long minutes with somber shapes moving around us, with everyone having a bite to eat and putting Le Goff out of their minds, Lazenec and I were like two stags in the forest watching each other, unsure whether or not to do battle.

But just as I was about to get my coat from the cloak-room, with Erwan already waiting for me on the porch and smoking, Lazenec quickly came over and started talking to me, the way he knew how to, about how what had happened was terrible, that between you and me, he said, I wouldn't have thought that Le Goff was so fragile.

I answered that yes, it was terrible, that's so, and I was already putting on my coat to leave when he took me aside, away from the crowd, adding some vague stuff—that in the world of politics it's a pity to have to say this, but you have to be tough; that maybe Le Goff had more of a dark side than was apparent—pushing the conversation further and further. I just acquiesced without saying anything be-cause in any case I didn't have any appropriate answers. I just shrugged a few times as if to say, I don't know anything about it, I'm sure he had his reasons, we never really know people, you know.

Deep inside, I was saying to myself: What do you want to know, Lazenec? What do you think I know, and why do you care? And for just a moment, it was as if I glimpsed the dark, naked shape of the demon in him, as if the shape had started dancing right under my nose, with all those well-turned phrases like a musical score. And I also said to my-self: Now I'm like a weed he'd want to rip out, a weed he's afraid is going to grow and keep growing back. We were in a standoff of silence and sentences with hidden meanings, as if we were pawns on a chessboard. A kind of local Yalta, right there in the grayish setting of the mayoralty, everything seemingly rearranged with a few handshakes, with him wondering what stake he could chain me to, as with a donkey, or goat, or beaten dog, without realizing that I was already out there, chained like the dog in the fable.

Chained to what? asked the judge. You weren't chained to anything, unless maybe it was your pride?

No, it wasn't pride. You don't know the feeling that still lurks deep inside us, a thing that's strange and unfathomable, absurd, you might say, of course absurd, but the worst is that we've made up a pretty word for that absurd thing hiding deep within that keeps us from just letting go, and that pretty word is "hope." I said this to the judge in just that way, in that tone of voice, so he would pick up the little quotation marks I put like a golden fringe around the word "hope."

Hope for what? he asked.

This time I looked him straight in the eye, as if claiming my right before any head of state. The hope of getting my money back, I said.

At that, the judge slumped in his chair, struck by what I'd said, like a spectator in an old movie theater wondering how soon the movie would end, or even if it ever would.

You don't know what it's like to have money on the brain, I said. It doesn't have anything to do with what you might do with it or what you may lack in your daily life, I mean if I could turn that money into some sort of material asset even for a moment, I would plop right down on it like an old pillow. But that's not it, it doesn't involve money as money, no, it has to do with a piece of flesh torn out, you understand, a piece of living flesh that burns on and on, as if Lazenec the cowboy had put me to sleep on an operating table and removed an organ, I don't know which one, maybe the heart, in any case something very important, that he took out of me and I haven't woken up since then, and it's only when I'll have found that organ again that I can get up and resume a normal and useful life. That's how, even when you feel that all is lost, even when you've quit looking to the future, you still face the steps of despair, and you go down them very slowly one by one, but never all at once. I swear, there's something in your brain that keeps you from racing down them.

So yeah, I waited for my money for nineteen hundred and fifty days, right up until yesterday, and I don't mean the return on my money, not those shiny percentages I'm sure I calculated over and over during the first five hundred days, no, it didn't take me that long to understand I would never get them, I'm talking about my initial stake, the five hundred and twelve thousand francs. I was still at that point, with the idea that you can always go back, like the Ferris wheel that magically started to go backward just when I thought it never would, that one day instead of this whole business being in my brain, there would be a blank page wiped clean by a magic eraser, so that when I would be out on my own Merry Fisher casting for bass, I could smile, thinking back on all this. But that's not how it works. I know that, now. And Lazenec probably knew it, too. So the only thing I could think to say, facing Lazenec with our glasses of cider that weren't sparkling anymore, the only thing I could say to end the conversation was: Monsieur Lazenec, don't you think you've gone too far this time?

It's almost strange, but just that simple sentence, that simple fake question, seemed to relieve him, as if in that phrasing, which was even more enigmatic than his, I was saying, You leave me alone and I'll leave you alone. And he sort of smiled, if you could call it a smile.

Do you mean a rictus? asked the judge.

I had to say no, that I knew the word "rictus," and if I'd needed to use it, of course I would have, but that it wasn't a rictus. A smile, I said.

Then I turned my back on Lazenec and went outside to join Erwan, who was finishing his cigarette and pacing in front of the glass doors with his head covered with the kind of hood that so cuts him off from the world. But I know he'd followed the whole scene. He didn't need be a lip-reader to judge the balance of power between Lazenec and me and to feel it, because when it comes to those things you have to be really naïve to think they can be wrapped in language made up of sentences, when any five-year-old can look at the slump of shoulders or the bow of a neck and tell which person has power over the other and could crush him single-handedly.

But Erwan didn't say anything, just started walking with that loose teenage stride where you don't know what to do with your body, hands in his pockets as if to say he was calm and unmoved, maybe, or maybe just the opposite, to hide his violence and nervous tension, fists clenched for sure, waiting for some evening bigger than the others, considering that all this was filling Erwan much more than me, as I've learned since.

What was filling him more than you?

The class struggle, I said. And for the first time since I'd stepped into the office and faced the judge, I smiled.

It wasn't for lack of telling Erwan lies, trying to lie to him for his own good, for the good of all of us, for social peace, you understand. On that rainy road, I said that everything would soon be all right, that I'd talked at length with Lazenec and lots of things would change soon, whereas I felt in my gut that I could just as well have begun with the only definite sentence worth saying, which was something like, "All right, your father is a moron, your father's been cheated up and down the line, and now he's crawling on his belly, and you're his son and you're seeing his fall." Just imagining saying this to my son, I felt all the weight that had been pressing down on me for so many years lift, as if I were descending a long series of steps toward a void, and deep in that void there might be an underground exit, a light that would appear in the bottom of a cave in which I would put down one by one all the weapons I'd kept as armor on my skin for so long. But I didn't say anything, of course. We just walked along in the damp silence.

It wasn't very far from the mayoralty to my place, less than a mile on the wet sidewalks to the château pathway, the former château, that is, but my house was still there, our house, like a border outpost in a country at war. You should come see someday, I told the judge. Photos aren't enough, you have to see what it looks like, that lonely house standing in the middle of a field of dirt, like it's lost in the mud. It's bad enough that it's so easy to get lost in these parts because of the heaviness of the clouds or, I don't know, the trees that look like a sort of mangrove swamp and seem to tumble into the sea. I'll take you out someday, there are places deep in the peninsula here that look like South America. I've never been to South America but I've seen things on television, I've seen muddy rivers with trees and their exhausted reflection in the gray water, and sometimes it's like that here, and then you feel that you could lose your soul, or at least that it could slip away between the tree branches, in the shades of green and the little stone walls along the bank, that it could lose itself in the flat expanses of stony dunes that seem to go on and on. You have to understand this, I told the judge. Once you're past the channel narrows, what takes your breath away isn't the open ocean or the strength of the wind but the stagnant water, the muddy smell you find in rivers, that's what the bottom of a harbor is like. In a way, the harbor is the ocean minus the ocean.

We reached our house's porch, looking at our solitude buried under all that excavated earth, and I remember saying to Erwan: Now I'd like grass to grow back, just that, grass that grows and hides stuff. But before seeding the grass, before erasing the scars in the earth, it would have to be cleaned up, I said.

Erwan was staring out to sea, aiming his gaze between the cliffs on either side of the harbor. Without blinking or turning his head a hundredth of a degree toward me, he just answered, "Yeah, there's lots of things that should be cleaned up."

We were like two actors who didn't dare face each other and instead looked at the audience, if the audience was the whole harbor, with the water, the sky, and the mud all watching and holding their breath. I looked out at the ocean as well, the fall of the rocks that you could barely make out with the rain dampening the sky, and I didn't turn my head a hundredth of a degree toward him either, since we were sharing our thoughts well enough in silence, when language itself is a useless luxury because there was nothing more to say, nothing more to understand, at least if understanding would mean making a sentence that uses "so" and "then" to articulate and clarify, but no, understanding inside, I told the judge, it's more like deeply feeling here, right here. I put my finger not on my heart or my chest but on my stomach below the solar plexus, yeah here, understanding that causes a pain people have known since antiquity, I swear, without being quite sure if it burns, or stings, or destroys.

The two of us stood dazed by the wind and the rain.

The two of us, still standing there facing the sea. Except that the sea was suddenly like an impasse. And among the few words he managed to pull from the silence, Erwan asked: What are you going to do now?

What do you expect me to do? I said. That kind of guy is like the rain, there's nothing else to do except wait for it to stop.

But do you think a seventeen-year-old kid can handle that without flinching? I asked the judge. No, of course not, so he kept on looking at the horizon, or rather the absence of horizon, and you know what he said, my own son, you know what he said, which he must have ruminated over for hours in fear and pain in his bedroom? Still without looking at me, he asked: Are you going to wind up like Le Goff?

I didn't answer. I couldn't. I was like an invisible shadow next to him, a lifeless and silent shadow that only wanted to soothe and comfort him, yes, even today I'd like to wrap him in my comforting, the same comforting that so clashed with—what?—his anger maybe or maybe his fear, and I'm the first to admit that I should have comforted him more often, stilled the wind that howled along the baseboards. Because now I understand that Erwan was like an electric battery that I'd been continuously charging all those years.

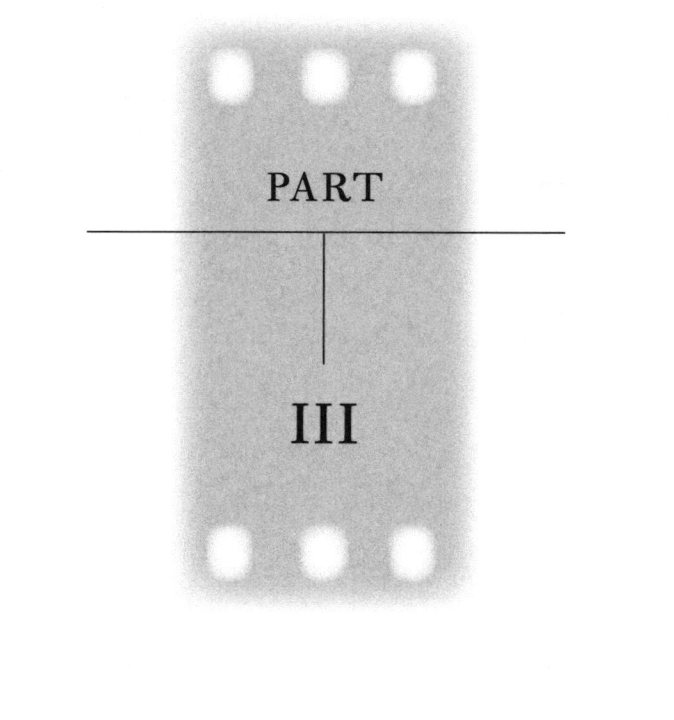

PART

III

I've gone to see him a lot recently. I've had time to ob-
serve him through the glass in the visiting room. I've noticed new wrinkles under his eyes and I thought, That's not
fatigue, he's just gotten older than his age, and it's basically
because of me. No. Not because of me. Because of Lazenec.
Lazenec, who testified against Erwan on the stand in the
courtroom. The same Lazenec who played up being a vic-
tim, which he was so good at, telling the court: "Violence
never solves anything, Your Honor. I may have my faults,
but I've never used violence to settle things."

And then I saw Erwan standing in the dock, about to
speak. I'll always remember that, I told the judge, when I
entered the courtroom and looked around to see him in the
defendant's box, handcuffed, leaning against the metal bar
that was like the prow of a ship, a little shiny in the overhead fluorescent lights and already damp from earlier verdicts. There were a lot of people on the wooden benches, as
if they'd come to the movies, and there was Erwan, standing alone in the light, not daring to look at me. Now that I
think of it, I can't say he really looked at me even once these

last weeks, during the many hours of court hearings and all those times in the visiting room.

From her dais, the trial judge opened the hearing by saying, Erwan Kermeur, do you acknowledge the facts you are charged with? And he in turn very clearly and calmly said, Yes, I acknowledge them.

Erwan then told the whole story, down to the smallest details: How he took my car keys from the buffet in the hallway and went out. How he drove without a license to the marina and parked there, by the chain-link fence around the work sites. How he walked around the warehouses to the basin that sheltered the sailboats and power boats. Though "sheltered" is overstating it; manhandled would be more like it: That night the wind was blowing so hard that the boats were being manhandled and shaken relentlessly. It might have been midnight, and there wasn't anyone there, only bad genies rising from the waves, popping up on every burst of white spray to whisper some evil plan into your ear. Imagine a November night with the wind blowing Force 8, nothing protecting anything, and the wind hissing faster than birds of prey screaming through the air. There was no one around, said Erwan, absolutely no one, otherwise I wouldn't have done it, of course.

He opened the little gate to Dock A marked "Reserved for Yachts," tried not to slip while walking down the iron gangway, and stepped onto the wooden dock amid the racket of colliding crosstrees and loose halyards banging against masts. You know that sound, don't you? The metallic clanging you can hear all the way up here when the wind blows from the north, like an orchestra that can't get in tune. So he stepped onto the dock and walked along the lights lining the pathways, his footsteps covered by the craziness of the wind whirling among the boats, and stopped in front of a Merry Fisher that probably hadn't been out for the past two months. He stood there looking at it, he told the trial judge, getting soaked by waves that the breakwater farther out was trying to control.

He stood there like that for a long time, just watching the boat moving, jerking against mooring lines tied to cleats forward, aft, and amidships, solidly anchored against times like this, when every extra inch you snug a line tighter helps you sleep at night when you're thinking about your boat. If it were my boat, I would have doubled the bow and stern lines and also the spring lines, to make absolutely sure it wouldn't move, and I'd still pray that nothing would come loose. But it wasn't my boat. It was Lazenec's. And Lazenec probably didn't pray hard enough stop a young idiot... Okay, I've called my son an idiot for once, and right in front of you. It's the first time, but I'm sure you can understand how good it feels to say something bad about your son. It's usually the other way around—it's supposed to be healthy for children to speak ill of their parents—but it actually works both ways, because of how crazily attached we are to them, so to sometimes let yourself believe your child is a person like anyone else, and to think you can have some effect on their reasoning and maybe even their judgment the way you might on some stranger's, really does one good.

So my son the idiot thought long and hard, weighing each move he was about to make. Then he bent down to the cleat bolted to the dock, took the salt-soaked mooring line, and began to untie it, calmly slipping the end through the loop to undo the knot, releasing the spring line that kept the boat from backing away from the dock. The sea told me to do it, he said, with all those waves pounding on our coast, all those mooring lines holding that awful Merry Fisher in the hard chop, it was like a wild horse tied up in its stall, desperate to get out, I swear, Your Honor, it was being so jerked around that it was whinnying on the water, I just had to do it.

And as I listened to him say this, with each image entering my mind so precisely, I was telling myself this can't be, he couldn't have done it. But of course he had. He did. He moved along the hull down the dock to the other mooring lines holding the boat, bent over to them one by one, and loosened each knot, releasing the lines holding the boat one after another, untying them, untying them in the storm.

And now the Merry Fisher was free.

I can imagine how the boat must've banged crazily against the wooden dock, unsure whether to go forward, rise in the air, or go backward, as if the boat itself were deciding anything, as if it were able to exercise some bit of self-determination. In reality, when the sea is at all rough, no boat, whether it belongs to Lazenec or some other idiot, can decide which way it will be tossed, not its nice clean hull or the four hundred horses resting in the raised twin outboard motors, nor what rock, breakwater, or hull it will hit first, now that it was like a child's bathtub toy shaken by all the gods of vengeance and justice combined, and would soon lie smashed on the shore, filling with water.

For a few minutes, sitting there in the courtroom, I enjoyed the sight of Lazenec listening to this, the wreck of his awful boat, even though he bought a new one the following day, the exact same Merry Fisher model, with the money from a shady insurer he had treated to white wine and abalone. But I swear that had no importance right then compared to that other pleasure, Erwan's, who went on telling what happened, like an indifferent machine mechanically cranking out his actions in order.

Because there was more to come.

Because it wasn't enough for him to see Lazenec's boat dancing on the water, no. Standing there on the dock, staring at all those boats like so many slaps in the face that awoke such pain in him, I don't know what came over him, but he started untying them all, one after another, all the Merry Fishers, the Antareses, and the other motorboats, working his way down the dock right to the end, thirty boats untied in the storm one after another, yes, he did that, and when he described it to the trial judge, he was almost smiling. He could still see them like little ducks, is what he said, little ducks in a bathtub starting to bang into each other, bumper cars discovering the mutual joy of colliding, all eager to join their big brother who had already washed up on the beach.

Front-page news, next day.

Every TV station in France came to shoot the same clip: thirty boats driven onto the beach by the current, piled up like in a junkyard, scattered by the power of the waves that had swept them up. Crowds on the railing, admiring the result. And every witness saying: We've never seen the like. Never seen the like.

The judge didn't stir. Between him and me, it was as if there were now a pile of little model boats on his desk.

It's true, I said, we'd never seen the like. But now you understand how the hundred thousand volts I've been pouring into him all these years, you understand how they were discharged.

I tried to explain that to the trial judge, too. The circumstances. Yes, the circumstances, I said. I'm not trying to win your sympathy, I said, but there are circumstances, after all.

Now holding on to the metal bar in my turn, I remember, the first thing I said to the trial judge facing me, in front of the full courtroom, was: Do you know La Fontaine's fables, Your Honor?

Unsure whether to smile or not, she simply said, "Go on." So I told her. Everything I knew. Everything you know,

now. The past six years. The château. The money. The emptiness. Erwan's childhood.

All I'm asking, I told her, is for you to believe me when I say that I took good care of Erwan. During all those years together I never let him hang out in the empty town alone, never left him at the bus stop with the other bored boys his age, spending long Saturday afternoons under the concrete shelter, not Erwan. To keep him from that, I took the car and we went for drives, we walked on the rocks, or sometimes just had a drink in the port looking at boats, yes, we often did that, looking at the boats on the docks. Now I wonder if that was the best thing I did.

I told the trial judge that I was wrong, that I'd done things backward, and that's probably the fate of parents, I said, it's the fate of parents to someday look back and be afraid that they'd failed. I'm not sure she quite understood what I wanted to say, since all I could come up with after that was a somewhat heavy silence—somewhat judgmental, actually as if I should've weighed what I'd just said, while I tried to catch the eye of someone to support me, maybe Erwan's, and especially France's. She was sitting all the way to the right on the other side of Erwan, with me at the bar in the middle. The three of us could've made a perfect triangle of which I was the top point, while the trial judge on her dais was across from me, you might say symmetrically, like a more powerful magnet, just by her presence drawing the point of the triangle to herself. And I felt that I should talk, that I should go on talking so the triangle of Erwan, France, and me, that triangle, wouldn't disappear completely.

Standing there at the courtroom bar, do you know what I felt like talking about in front of the crowd? Maybe because of the cold of the metal bar I was leaning against, as I looked at Erwan and France, what I felt like talking about was the day I wound up hanging from the car of the Ferris wheel, dangling in space, and watching Erwan's hands gripping my wrists, trying to get around my wrists, yes, I wanted to talk about that. But I didn't. All I said was: Your Honor, none of this is Erwan's fault. Erwan just wanted to keep me from falling.

And I'm not sure that it was actually her I was speaking to at that moment, since my gaze kept moving from the center to the right, toward France and her eyes, and of course she was looking away, probably doing everything she could to keep from cursing me, and even then in the courtroom, it's strange sometimes when two people's eyes are trying so hard not to meet, sometimes each person knows that they're seeking and magnetizing the other, as if they'd drawn a fluorescent line where they refused to meet, like a reversed magnetic field, like two magnets repulsing each other but which you kept trying to bring together, that was France and me, both of us, as if we were both to blame and it went back to the very fact of our being parents.

When the verdict was handed down the next day, and Erwan was sentenced to two years in prison for aggravated vandalism, property damage, and disturbing the peace, the two years in prison seeming to darken the very beams supporting the ceiling, France left right away. The moment she heard the total of days woven like a net around Erwan, I saw her get up and leave, like a reporter who might've just come to cover the event, at least that's what she would've liked it to look like, and not a mother torn up inside, unable to sit in her chair another minute, unable to imagine her son behind the glass of a visiting room, but instead an indifferent reporter doing her job, anything so as not to collapse in the courtroom crying "Erwan" or "Martial," as she might have needed to do.

A hubbub rose in the courtroom, a general end-of-session movement, Erwan motionless in his box, people's whispered comments. So I went out too, and the two of us, France and me, found ourselves in the courthouse hallway under the big windows facing the sea. We sat down on a bench without saying anything, without even judging if the sentence was heavy or light, or simply fair. France didn't say anything, looking at the worn floor tiles, but then she did, at last she said, This is your fault. Maybe it was just once, but once is enough to cut down a man like me and raise an inner army of guilt. Maybe she didn't really mean it, maybe it was because she was angry or upset, but it's always too late, she said it once and it's written there, inside my skull, I swear this time when I heard that, it felt like my whole scalp had been pulled back, ripping everything raw, and rubbing alcohol poured directly onto my brain.

And if I were able to answer her, if I'd had the strength to make conversation, if I were only able to say anything, it would be with my gasping breath that she would hear not what I really had to say but the very fact that I couldn't say anything. I think she understood some things in my silence.

At least that's the way I interpreted it when she stood up a little later and then, as she was leaving—because it's always when you're leaving that these things happen, as if you're already gone, you understand, and the fact of your no longer being there, as if you had the right to do things that you would never dare when you were still all there, the right to say things in confidence when you're already on your feet—we were standing in the open big glass door, and I could already feel the air on her neck pulling her outside, as we parted, we joined hands, yes, just our hands, and maybe it was a second longer, I mean, we held hands a second longer and then I don't know what happens at moments like that, but I know that she and I squeezed each other's hands a little harder and then we stepped very close to each other and, yes, we kissed, we kissed each other long enough for me to remember what that felt like to kiss her, before she kind of jerked and slowly backed away, and then, see, she left.

As I left the courthouse, standing outside on the few outdoor steps above the harbor, I tried to take stock of where I was, the way you sometimes can in life, where you want to note all the coordinates, where you use a compass on a chart to measure distances and landmarks, and draw a little x in pencil on the paper: "Here's where I am." Except that now the landmarks weren't just steeples or water towers standing like beacons over the ocean anymore but instead were dry, solitary sentences, averted faces, and "it's your fault" or "your son." I remember the seagull that was standing there, with the calm ocean stretching away in front of us. Then Erwan came out of the courthouse, head down, pushed by the policemen into the car that would take him to the jail where he was being held.

I watched the car drive off, the nape of Erwan's neck just visible through the rear window, and I kept telling myself: Something's wrong, something's backward in this life. In a normal world I would be the one there, in the back of a white sedan with "Police" written on it, not Erwan, not my seventeen-year-old son.

That happened right here, Your Honor, in this very courthouse a few floors down. It's as if everything was converging here from the beginning, like, I don't know, a painting you might look at from anywhere but that keeps pulling you back to the center, as if I were drawn by a light that would always bring me here. Maybe you're the light, I told the judge, maybe you magnetize my memories and set them spinning in me like the rings around Saturn.

Maybe so, said the judge, maybe so.

You know, I think this courthouse remembers everything. I think it holds all the trials and the verdicts in the world, silently and methodically storing them deep inside, for centuries. I think that one day, when it collapses, on that day it'll suddenly spit out all of the injustices on earth and they'll spread like a black cloud over the cities of the future. But the problem, I told the judge, is that I won't be around to see it. Not me or anybody else in this story. And Lazenec no more than the others.

So you understand that one can't always wait for centuries for some sort of natural justice that might never be done.

Lazenec came out then, surrounded by reporters asking for his reactions, microphones held to his silent mouth, and maybe the reporters were thinking the same thing I was, that the world was upside down, that the only person who should've left under a flashing blue police light was him. He passed by me but didn't see me. I watched him get into his car in the parking lot, and I had the feeling I would never see him again.

Obviously I was wrong, I said to the judge.

With a guy like that, if you don't get rid of him, he'll never disappear, that's what I've come to understand, Your Honor. He'll come back. Always. Basically that's all he knows how to do, come back; he slips away of course, but then comes back, hidden in the shadow of a clock that measures weeks instead of hours, maybe waiting for us to be less angry, waiting for me to get over the bad nights I spent ruminating and telling myself that it wasn't his boat that Erwan should've gone after. I can't tell you how many days or weeks passed, or even how many times I visited Erwan at the jail on Wednesday afternoons. But I know that in those thirty weekly minutes we spent facing each other there, it was as if I were gradually taking back the hundred thousand volts that were still humming inside him, I was positively filling myself with all of Erwan's dark energy and soon, yes soon, I would be charged up enough to put everything right.

But the days slip by and accumulate like silt that slows the current. Time, time that was once bitter and nervous and sleepless, becomes smooth and polished, like a layer of stones on the beach. And that was the moment Lazenec chose to come back as if nothing had happened—because nothing was finished, and nothing could ever finish because nothing had ever begun, you understand?

Lazenec rang my doorbell.

Three months, maybe. He lasted three months without being seen in any street in town and without coming to inspect his five acres of mud, just three months, and then he rang my bell.

What kind of a brain, I asked the judge, what brain do we normal people need to have to recognize that there's a category of people like that on earth, who lack that thing I'm sure you and I share, I told the judge, something that normally stops us or threatens us, something—a conscience maybe—that arises pretty early, provided we have the shaky mirror in our heads that made even Adam cover himself with a fig leaf, something that hobbles us, yes, but also honors us. And the fact is that some people lack that thing, the way others are born without an arm, and others are born lacking, I don't know, lacking...

Humanity? said the judge.

Yes, basically that's it, humanity.

So here's the guy who destroyed Le Goff, the guy who destroyed Erwan, the guy who destroyed me, this same guy shows up at my door and acts like he's an ordinary neighbor who might've come by just to say hello or, I don't know, out of amnesia, trying to smooth over the past the way you varnish a floor to avoid splinters, and he says, mechanically: I'm sorry about Erwan.

I don't think I knew what to say.

If I can ever be helpful, he continued, let me know.

No, I said, I don't think so.

And Lazenec did that sort of quarter-turn when someone is on the point of leaving but already knows that he's not going to go before he follows his thought to the end, and he stopped and looked at me and said: If you like, we could go fishing together one of these days.

Beg pardon? I said.

I could take you out, he said. And he added: I don't bear grudges.

You hear that? I asked the judge. He said that: I don't bear grudges. Five hundred twelve thousand francs and he's the one who doesn't bear grudges, what in the world can a guy like me say to that? With the darkness, or evil, or malevolence that guys like him use to stab at the people around them, somehow, in some way I can't explain to you, they manage to take away whatever dignity people have left, or maybe just their common sense.

Because here's the thing: I said yes.

The rest, you know.

The rest was written by the currents that wash bodies up on our coast. You can call it voluntary homicide or some expression or other that says things in a normal language, but what I did, Your Honor, doesn't make me feel like a killer, what I did was to ostracize him, you understand, I ostracized him the way you burn off a wart to grow new skin. It was as if the skin were our town and the time had come to pull the evil out by the root. I did it for the good of all of us.

The sun now seemed to be breaking through, maybe because of the turning of the tide at five o'clock. When the tide turns, the weather here often changes and the sky clears up around five, in any case you see the sun more often in the afternoon than in the morning, there's no explaining it but that's the way it is.

Anyway, I didn't really kill him. In terms of finishing him off physically, the sea did a lot better job than I did, but as for justice... Justice, I told the judge, only people can do that.

But the fact is, he's dead, said the judge. The fact is, you're the one sitting here facing me.

What do you mean?

The sea and the fog won't be on trial, you will.

Yes, but so what? What do you expect me to do about it?

No one can ignore the law, said the judge.

No, of course not, no one can ignore the law, I said. If we forgot about it, if we erased it from the law books, everything would crumble, right? And those books of yours standing on the shelves, you could toss them all out the window. With a little luck, you'd see them floating in the harbor. With a little luck, the fish would read them. But I think you'll agree that the fish and the seaweed don't need to read books like that, because they're not about to ignore the laws that concern them.

There was another silence, and then I said: Is this going to cost me big-time?

I don't know, he said.

You don't know?

No, it depends.

On what?

On me.

Suddenly he stood up, as if he couldn't sit still anymore, or wanted to get out of his judge's armchair, and walked over to the window with his hands in his pockets. Then he turned back to me, maybe hesitating one last time, and using a tone as if he were asking me a question, said: After all, this outing of yours on the water, it could also have been an accident.

I frowned, trying to understand what he meant, that is, understanding perfectly what he meant to say but maybe not unfolding it into a logical, organized sentence, more like a ball of fire ricocheting through my brain from one side to the other, unsure what wall it would stop at. It was odd to see the judge deliberately look down and start playing with the end of his necktie, without knowing if this was the pride of someone who's holding all the strings or the awkwardness of someone thinking he was going beyond the law, so I just said: For me, this isn't a laughing matter, Your Honor.

As he stood there looking at me, stroking his chin and letting the silence last, I understood that he wasn't joking.

But I should've gone to get help, I said, or maybe run to the harbormaster's office, so an accident... You know that there are a lot of things against me, Your Honor.

But the judge was no longer listening to me. He now took one of the red books lying on his desk and opened it in front of him, as if now only law books could decide the matter, as if everything I'd said during those long hours sitting there, everything I was saying now to lighten this end of the day, I hadn't said to a judge or the courthouse air, but that each sentence had just been waiting to take its place there, on the pages of a law book.

Amid the rustling of that same paper, which he gently leafed through, the judge found the page he was looking for, ran his finger down it, stopped, and said, Listen carefully, Kermeur, listen carefully and maybe this will make it clearer for you.

And then he started reading aloud, calmly and distinctly, like he was addressing a big crowd, or because he wanted me to learn each sentence by heart, and I heard him read:

Article 353 of the Penal Code: The law does not ask judges to account for the ways they reach decisions, and it does not prescribe rules by which they must particularly weigh the sufficiency or adequacy of evidence; it requires that they determine in silence and contemplation and in the sincerity of their conscience what impression the evidence against the accused and the means of that person's defense have made on their thinking. The law asks of them only this one question, which contains the full measure of their duty: Are you fully convinced?

Now, when I look at the sea from my kitchen window, when I breathe the free air of the sea below, I often recite the lines of Article 353 aloud, like a psalm from the Bible written by God himself, in the judge's voice, which still echoes in my ears as he looked at me more intently than ever, and said: An accident, Kermeur, an unfortunate accident.

TANGUY VIEL was born in Brest, France, in 1973. He is the author of seven novels, including *Le Black Note*, *Cinéma*, *The Absolute Perfection of Crime* (winner of the Prix Fénéon and the Prix littéraire de la Vocation), *Beyond Suspicion*, *Paris-Brest*, and *La Disparition de Jim Sullivan*. *Article 353* won the Grand prix RTL-Lire 2017 and the Prix François-Mauriac de la région Aquitaine. He lives near Orléans, France.

WILLIAM RODARMOR has translated some forty-five books and screenplays in genres from literary fiction to espionage and fantasy. In 1996, he won the Lewis Galantière Award from the American Translators Association for *Tamata and the Alliance* by Bernard Moitessier. In 2017 he won the Northern California Book Award for fiction translation for *The Slow Waltz of Turtles* by Katherine Pancol. He lives in Berkeley, California.

HOLD FAST YOUR CROWN by Yannick Haenel

An exasperated writer obsessed with American cinema embarks on an increasingly bizarre journey in this heady, engrossing novel.

"Crazy, brilliant, addictive, and darkly poetic."
—*Le Figaro*

"Wonderfully mad." —*Le Parisien*

THE PARTING GIFT by Evan Fallenberg

An erotic tale of jealousy, obsession, and revenge, and a shrewd exploration of the roles men assume, or are forced to assume, as lovers, as fathers, as Israelis, as Palestinians.

"An erotic, mysterious novel."
—*New York Times Book Review*

"An unabashed tale that does not pull punches and looks at love's underside…hits hard and never lets up."
André Aciman, author of *Call Me by Your Name*

THE REPUBLIC by Joost de Vries

A biting academic satire about deception and self-deception, ambition, and the hunt for the perfect enemy. This novel immerses us in the world of the global intelligentsia, where the truth counts for less than what is said about it.

"An uncompromisingly intellectual novel that can just as easily be called a matchless social comedy."
—Arnold Heumakers, *NRC Handelsblad*

Also recommended:

SOMETHING GREAT AND BEAUTIFUL: A NOVEL OF LOVE, WALL STREET, AND FOCACCIA by Enrico Pellegrini

NAMED A *BOOK RIOT* BEST BOOK OF 2018

"Must-read." —*New York Post*

"Both a love story and a witty indictment of the boom-or-bust cycles of the financial world, *Something Great and Beautiful* is an enjoyable, almost mythical tale written with flair and searing insight." —*Booklist*

THREE FLOORS UP by Eshkol Nevo

FINALIST FOR TWO 2017 NATIONAL JEWISH BOOK AWARDS

"Eshkol Nevo is a fascinating storyteller who gives the reader a broad and diverse picture of Israeli society." —Amos Oz, bestselling author of *Judas*

"Mesmerizing…this book and its conflicted apartment dwellers stayed with me long after I finished reading." —*New York Times Book Review*

QUICKSAND by Malin Persson Giolito

NAMED AN NPR BEST BOOK OF 2017

NAMED THE BEST SWEDISH CRIME NOVEL OF THE YEAR BY THE SWEDISH CRIME WRITERS ACADEMY

"This is the evolution of Scandinavian crime, in more ways than one." —Fredrik Backman, author of *A Man Called Ove*

"A remarkable new novel…[Giolito] writes with exceptional skill…[*Quicksand* is] always smart and engrossing…Giolito keeps us guessing a long time and the outcome, when it arrives, is just as it should be." —*Washington Post*

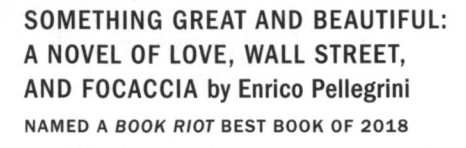

OTHER PRESS   *www.otherpress.com*